Acknowledgements

First I would like to thank my cat Sam for being a helpful furry supporter. I'd like to think him and Wolfe would have been best friends.

I would like to thank my friends and those of the community that have been supportive and anticipated for the release of *The Demonic Eyes*. They know who they are.

Special appreciation to the current and past staff of the Russell Memorial Library. They have been part of the amazing journey since my young age of three, showing me all that books have to offer: Tonya Revell, Jayme Viveiros, Constance "Connie" Preston, Denise Charland, Pauline Prudhomme, and Sandra "Sandy" Medeiros.

Additionally, I owe thanks to the amazing Scott Blagden (author of *Dear Life, You Suck*) who helped guide me in the right path on how to get my novel out there and all of his helpful critiquing advice.

Of course I wouldn't have done it without Page Publishing, so a great thank you to them:

Also a special thanks to my photographer Michael Cloutier.

Many thanks to my past and future teachers that have contributed to my education.

Lastly, my biggest appreciation goes to my mother who has always supported me throughout my writing. Without her, you would not be holding the book in your hands that you are now.

So the dice rolls turning on its side. Evens are for good. Odds are for evil.

—Damian Winters

MONTHS AFTERWARD

Blood was the first thing I saw when I regained my self-control. I was drenched in the dark crimson; it stained my clothing and lips. The warmth filled my mouth. An addictive poison. I craved to taste more. The blood splattered the walls, traveled throughout the floor in a river, and seeped through my boot soles. I dropped the blade in my hand, my mouth agape.

Below me was a person lying in a dark puddle. His eyes were black, dilated, and lifeless, staring right through me. Slices marked his wrists, neck, and chest. His frozen heart exposed, he bled to death.

I couldn't remember how many times it had been that I had repeatedly stabbed the victim. All I could remember was one moment killing, the next moment not understanding what I had done. *What have I done? This can't be me.* But it was.

I turned my head and saw her standing there unmoving. Anyone else would have been terrified. Not her. She was one with the darkness, and now so was I.

My bottom lip began to tremble—not wanting to be this way, but there was no choice. What I did was supposed to be considered for the better. So why did I feel so guilty, afraid? Through all my years, I had never felt anything this terrifying. I was a monster. I became everything I wished to never become.

"It's okay," she said. "It's hard the first time." Some blood had gotten on her cheek, but she didn't bother to wipe it away. "We are safe now. Everything will be okay."

She went up to me and wrapped her arms around me, splotching her shirt with blood. We stayed like that for a long time, standing there, hugging in silence. She then pressed her soft lips against mine, trying to tell me what she couldn't put into words.

What she said was not true for I knew what was. We had to leave, escape together before everything gets worse. The war never stops for long. There is always a new enemy no matter where you turn.

So the dice rolls, turning on its side. Odds are for evil. Evens are for good.

THE NIGHT WANDERER

Months before

DAMIAN

The first time I saw her, it was a dark midnight. I had been walking down the street from the local gas station with a bag of gummy bears and an energy drink. Only a real loon would be out at this time. Well, I guess that is what I was, a loon. Sometimes I would just escape out of the house in the middle of the night and walk around town. At night there was practically no one around. I could be alone, not have to be so cautious of dreadful small talk. God, I hated people.

I was a misanthropic vampire. The daylight, I tried to avoid. It was happily irritating, and people were just wastes of space. They give me dirty looks all the time. At this hour, I didn't have to deal with their bullshit. People seemed to ignore one another, and the air was cool, quiet, and just right. The sense of peace made me feel sane.

If anyone I had known had ever seen me outside at that time, I would notice. Elders would rat me out to my father, and people my age would do just what they did every day. For those reasons I kept a low profile. I went and walked to places most people I knew wouldn't be like tonight.

I had been walking to the park where the benches stood. When I got there, I would sit upon one of them and look up at the stars far above me.

That idea was ruined though, as I had been walking upon the sidewalk. A car had pulled up beside me. A puddle of water splashed from underneath the tires. The water had missed my black sneakers by an inch, falling to the sidewalk. The car was a new 2008 Chevy Camaro red convertible model. It was a nice car, which made me believe the person driving it had only had stopped for directions as it had passed through the town. To the people of Stonebrook, that was one expensive car. No one who lived here could afford a ride like that except for maybe one family I greatly resented.

When the car came to a stop, the tinted window on the driver's side rolled down, revealing the person sitting behind the wheel. He was a man in about his late thirties with dark brown hair and dark eyes. Sitting next to him, in the passenger's seat, was a girl my age. I couldn't tell much about her through the darkness of the night.

"Hey," said the man, "sorry if I splashed any water on ya. I was wondering if you could help us."

"That's okay. Sure," I said though I wasn't a fan of helping others.

"Do you live around here?"

"Yeah," I answered, not wanting to lie. These people were obviously newbies, so there was no reason to.

"Perhaps you know where Charleston Street is. You see, we are just moving into town, and we don't quite know where it is," said the man.

I had instructed him where to go, and he thanked me. The man was about to drive away when he added, "Say, aren't you kind of young to be outside at this time of night? Look, I'm not some cop. I can't tell you what to do, but I used to do what you're doing. Maybe you're not hurting anybody. You seem like a nice boy. Believe me, I know kids who walk around the street at this time. They're not like you. My advice is to go home soon. I would if I were you. The cops might be doing their late night patrols. If they find you, they could mistake you for the wrong kind of kid."

"How do you know I'm not up to no good," I said, finding him quite strange.

"Your breath," he said. "Your eyes aren't dilated. You aren't walking funny, and you can process everything I'm saying. Take my advice. Go home, go to bed like normal kids should, and your parents will never question where you were. They won't argue with you on the fact you left the house without telling them. You won't get grounded, and you won't hear them saying what they had assumed you were doing. You won't have to take a drug test either. I saw a cop car pull out of the station not long ago. If I were you, I'd hurry."

"Okay," I responded, wondering who the hell this guy thought he was.

"Have a nice night…"

"Damian Winters," I said, shaking the man's outstretched hand.

"Tom Johansson," said the man. "I guess we'll see you around?"

"Yeah," I agreed, and the car speeded away.

I took his advice and went home that night. I didn't know why. It hadn't been any of his business what I had been doing, but perhaps Tom was right. Everyone thought I was a troublemaker. Just because I seemed to be the type of person that caused havoc doesn't mean it's true.

When I got home, I climbed up the tree outside my house and slid through the window into my room. Everything was dark in there, causing me to almost trip on something. After I had regained my balance, I opened the bedroom door to see if anyone had suspected a thing. Someone had, but it was not who I thought. There sitting before the door was a black cat with the bushiest tail you would ever see. Her big green eyes stared at me in what looked like anger. That silly cat always looked mad with its crazy fur about its face. As I looked at her, Wolfe meowed, baring sharp canine teeth.

"You silly cat," I said whispering, not knowing how long she had actually been sitting there. I assumed it was for a while. "Come on."

The cat slipped into my room, and I closed the door. After undressing, I hopped into bed. Wolfe fell asleep at my feet, purring loudly as my mind drifted away, as it often did, from the world. Tonight though was not your average night.

In my dream, I had been walking on the yellow lines of a concrete road. No cars sped by for everything seemed so vacant. A forest surrounded me to my left and right. Within it the sound of coyotes crying to the full moon was heard. This made Wolfe, who had been walking beside me, jump. The hair on her back stood on end, and she hissed loudly.

"It's okay," I said, but the cat didn't stop.

As I looked in front of me, there stood a figure. He was wearing a pair of jeans and a black hoodie that covered most of his face. It was dark; his face shadowed. By the muscular arms and by his stance, I knew the figure could only be male. I could tell he was staring at me for he stood there unmoving. Though I could not see the figure's face, I could just make out the sight of blood dripping down his chin.

"I'm coming for you, Damian." His voice was like daggers cutting through my skin. "You're next."

My awakening the next morning was not out of fear but because I had felt something. On my cheek lingered the feeling of sandpaper being rubbed against it. When my eyelids opened, I saw that it was Wolfe's tongue pressed against my skin.

Time to get up, she was saying. *Time for food.*

"You think you're a dog, don't you?" I asked, my arms flexing above my head.

Rolling out of bed, I then escaped from my room. The bell on Wolfe's collar danced about as she followed me down the stairs. Coming to the first floor, I strolled into the kitchen to find a note on the fridge door. I removed the magnet to read it. The note said:

Dear Damian,

I was called into work today. Sorry bud. I was really hoping to spend time with you. I don't know…go for lunch or something. I feel like we've been too distant for a while now. Ever since…well you know. I can't change that son. I wish I could as much as you do, but there is no such thing as a time machine. Is there? Look maybe another time. Son, I love you and I know we've had some differences. But I realize you are the way you are and there is nothing I can do to change that. I don't want to wind up losing you like I lost her one day and realize it was my fault that I didn't do anything to stop it. I want to know you kiddo. I want to understand who you are and maybe I'll learn to be your friend again.

Have a good day,
Dad

P.S: Don't be lazy. Do something constructive besides that art you do. Go hang out with your friends or something.

    I didn't know how to react to the letter he left me. It hadn't sounded like my father at all. It was as if he actually cared about my feelings for once. Did he really want to reconnect with me or was this just one of his moods? Was he actually realizing who I was? Probably not. For if he ever cared to know me, he would know I had no friends. Who would like someone like me?

    There was so much that went on between both of us that I just didn't know if we could ever be father and son again even if I tried. Maybe I will, but it wasn't going to help anything. I hadn't had a real heart-to-heart conversation with him since, well, a long time. It might have been years. I couldn't seem to remember. He didn't get me, didn't understand me just like everyone else. He probably didn't even know what I dealt with every day. If I told him, would he even care? I mean he is my father; he should care yet I felt doubtful.

    I told myself not to think of these things now. You see, the quiet ones always have the loudest minds. Sometimes it's just hard to control especially mine. So many thoughts run through my head all at once.

The questions, comments all confuse me until I'm put in a state. It's a state of mind that is hard to describe in words. It's the one when you don't know what you are, who you are. It's the state of mind in which confusion twists into a knotted ball of string. When you can't grasp what is reality or fiction.

I filled the paper and rolled it up. I licked it shut and put it between my lips. I gave it a light and smirked as the letter's ends slowly blackened.

A meow came from below me. It was Wolfe still waiting for that food. I don't know why animals enjoy the things that they eat, but she chowed it down as she wagged her tail in glee. I swore that cat thought she was a dog. Maybe she had been dropped on her head when she was younger just like me.

Not wanting to deal with memories, I plugged my MP3 into the speaker device, blasting Arctic Monkeys throughout the house. It was one of my favorite bands, which made me feel better. That morning as I made myself omelets, it would hopefully be a good day.

THE NEIGHBOR ACROSS THE STREET

MRS. HENDERSON

I had been watching the *Price Is Right* on that October morning when I had heard the sound of a truck backing into a driveway. I was disturbed by the sound, but at least my hearing aids were working properly again. Getting my cane, I limped over to the window. As I peered through the curtain, I could see a U-Haul truck in the driveway of the house next to the Winters' residence.

Seeing this had shocked me so. There hadn't been a person living in that house for fifty years. Now we were getting new neighbors. It was a delight, or at least I hoped it would be. Back in the day when I was a youngster, everyone was kind to one another. Now people were so rude (except for two folks in this town).

One of them came at the moment I peered out. A little white van with a giant logo upon it rode up next to the sidewalk. A person came out dressed in a uniform, a bag slugged around their shoulder and mail in hand. Seeing him, I walked over to the door.

The man's name was Will Patrick. He was a nice young lad in his late forties. He was our town mail deliverer and had been giving me my mail every morning except Sunday's for twenty years now. He always seemed to have a smile on his face and loved being social. With Will, it felt like I finally had the grandson I never had. Will was always there when you needed a hand.

"Hello, Mrs. Henderson," said the man as he came toward me. "My, what happened to you?"

"Oh, I'm old," I said with a laugh. "Things happen. I sprained my hip. Nearly broke it."

"Ooh, that's not good," commented Will. "I hope you feel better."

"I hope so too, Will. Say, have I gotten new neighbors?"

Will turned his head and looked across the street at the U-Haul. "Yeah. The Johansson family. They just moved into town today. I met them earlier. A father, son, and a daughter. Nice but definitely… different."

"Not from around these parts, I suppose?" I asked.

"Nope. They say they come from…I don't quite remember. I think they said either California or Florida. I don't know. Somewhere warm, I suppose."

"Been a long time since that house was filled," I said, the memories of the past flowing back to me. Deep, dark memories. "I remember it like yesterday."

"It has," said Will, handing me my mail, eyes full of concern. "Don't work yourself up over it now. Memories belong in the past, don't they? We got to keep moving forward."

"You're right, Will. How young are they?"

"The girl is Damian's age, and the boy, I suppose, is not much younger. Maybe a year or two."

"Oh," I said. "Well, maybe he'll have a new friend."

Damian was a delight, but he had some issues. I could tell for he always seemed to have this sad look in his eyes. I knew one of the reasons why. Everyone in this town had to know at this point. One day I had overheard some kids riding by on their bikes calling Damian something, probably taunting him for the incident years ago. What nerve!

Damian was very reserved from what I knew and very respectful. He would visit me every now and then (about once or twice in a month) and show me the art he did or something along the lines. He never talked about his life or school. Very discreet he was, but I didn't understand why.

His father, on the other hand, I didn't talk to very often. In fact, I don't ever recall having a conversation with the lad. He may have said hi as he jogged by or was getting in his car for work a few times. That was it. He was never home from what I could tell. He was very busy man, always on the job.

"Well, have a good day, Mrs. Henderson," said Will.

"You too," I said and went back into my house as Will walked to the van. I made sure to get one last glance at the house across the street.

NOT SO ALONE

Damian

When I put my plate into the sink, I heard a loud beeping sound. I looked outside the tiny kitchen window and saw a truck backing up into the next-door driveway. For a moment I was dumbfounded then the event of last night popped into my mind. This couldn't be them, but it was! Perhaps they stayed at the motel on Charleston Street for the night. Why this house though?

I dropped the subject, focusing on my own life and got dressed. I had no idea what to do with myself today. It wasn't like I had any friends to hang out with. Still, I didn't want to spend another day locked in my room, drawing and listening to music. Even though it sounded tempting, I did it all the time. I needed some change.

Coffee sounded good to me. I couldn't make coffee for my life. It always came out tasting terrible, but perhaps it was the type of coffee itself. It was decidedly so that coffee was the answer.

"Bye, Wolfe," I said going toward the front door.

"Meow," she said in response, which probably meant *How dare you leave me here alone.*

I grabbed my Batman hoodie and left. When everything was secure, I walked down the street, making sure to glance at the house next door.

The house was bigger than mine and possibly very expensive back in the day. Nobody had been in that house for decades. I never knew why very few people did. The house did have a few problems with it. Some of the windows were broken. The white paint had turned grey and was starting to peel off the house. Also some part of the porch was broken in a few places. I was surprised the realtors didn't fix that, but I guess the new neighbors didn't care.

I could not see any sight of the Johanssons as I walked by, but then again it was a little distant. The only people I saw were two guys bringing a sofa into the house. I had no idea why someone would want to live there. It was so out of shape. It was originally built in the 1800s. Unlike other houses, it was made of something different like cement or marble. It looked like it was part of a horror movie, about a witch in a house or something like that. That's why they said sometimes that a dead witch lived there, but it is just a bunch of street talk bullshit.

It didn't take long for me to get to Danny's Coffee Shop. It was the best place for coffee in town. I came there ever so often. The owner's name is Kyle. He opened the coffee shop a few years back. He had named it after his daughter Danny, who had died of cancer two years before he opened. She had only been seven years old.

When I entered the coffee shop, I was surprised to see the line wasn't as long as usual. Some people sat at tables drinking coffee and reading or busy with their laptops. There behind the counter was Miles, Kyle's only son. He was older than me at the age of twenty-three. He was a nice guy who actually understood me. Black-and-white tattoos marked his arms. He had gauges in his ears, which the lady in front of me couldn't help but criticize, and a black Mohawk hairstyle. When he saw me walk in, he smiled.

"Hey, Damian," he said. "Haven't seen you in a while. What can I do for you?"

"A cup of hot coffee, please. The way I usually take it."

"Coming up," he said as he turned to the coffeemaker machine. "So what have you been up to, Damian? Anything new?"

"Not much. Everything is just the same old thing."

"That's what I used to say when I was your age. Things will get better," said Miles, putting the cup on the counter before me.

I paid him what the drink had cost then asked, "What about you?"

"Last year of college, man. Wow, probably makes me sound old." He laughed a little. and I smirked. "After that, I'll start doing my dream career. Make money and eventually meet someone, have a family of my own. This year is probably the last year you'll see me here in Stonebrook. Being stuck in this little dumb town all my life, I just want to go out there, ya know. Explore the world."

"Sounds good, Miles. I know what it's like. I've never even been out of this crappy state," I said then took a sip of my coffee.

"You know what, we should meet up sometime, talk, hang out, you know. I feel like I don't know you as well as I should. You're a cool kid. Less complicated than other teenagers I've talked to. Hell, it's like we understand each other," said Miles, which had shocked me a little. He pulled out a post-it note and a pen. After writing down his number, he handed it to me. "Call me. We'll catch up."

"Okay, Miles," I said. "We sure will. See ya."

"See ya, man."

I slipped the number in my pocket and headed for the door. A good-bye came from behind me. I did not look back as I left the building. Eyes were upon my neck, the lingering feeling of a blade on my back. A knife through my back was expected, but it did not come. I could feel it like I did every time I entered or left a room. They were the eyes of those foul, judging humans. This time though, one was full of glee.

It felt a little too good to be true that I had made a friend that afternoon. Maybe there were people like me in Stonebrook after all. Those that were proud of who they are even if it seemed wrong. Maybe so or maybe not so much. I never really knew. There was not much I knew about Miles except for his family and his dreams. And no one ever seemed to notice him as a person, his goals and dreams, but by his appearance. I mean no one else was like him in the stupid-ass town of Stonebrook. Out of the twenty thousand people, could we really be alone?

I didn't get home too quickly for I was enjoying the atmosphere. The air was cool with its October breeze, just the way I liked it. The way it felt upon my skin was just right, not too cold like the December frost. It was relaxing in a sense, the way it tingled on your cheeks. The change of temperature made me feel not human, dead, cold, and numb.

As I walked down the street, words and pain all came tumbling back. They always did more than usual these days. I couldn't stop it. People say those thoughts; memories only come at night slipping into your dreams. That's a lie. They come back whenever they want to as if they think they can control you. It was as if I was a puppet on strings, doing whatever the voices in my head say. They were picking away at me like a miner in a coal mine. The only difference between day and night is that at night, it always got louder. So loud to the point I couldn't think straight, couldn't sleep. With the nightly walks, for some reason, the peace of it made the nasty voices go away but not for long. It didn't always work; sometimes they still stayed.

I pushed the thoughts away from me, heading toward the same spot I had met the Johanssons at. On the street, the puddle of water had evaporated, leaving the road dry. I kept walking on the sidewalk, past the spot, past the gas station, past dozens of houses until I had gotten home.

I paid no attention to the Johanssons new house as I walked into my own home. The rest of the day, I was alone.

THROUGH THE LOOKING GLASS

Viper

I had just happened to glance outside my window to see the Winters' boy as he had entered his home. He had black hair that came to the end of his neck with bangs that seemed to dangle over his right eye. Every part of the clothing he wore was black. He had even painted his nails that color, which made his skin seem even paler than it probably was. His lips were the perfect shade of pink. His eyes I couldn't see, but I assumed them to be blue. He was different from any other boy I had ever known in real life. The name Damian Winters suited him perfectly.

    I had come from a small town even smaller than this one. The population was half the size of this place and had no shops compared to here. There had been no supermarkets whatsoever in that town, causing you to go to a different one for your needs. People weren't too friendly either, especially the girls my age. They were fake, no doubt

THE DEMONIC EYES

about it. They all acted pretty much the same way, which I could only describe as fake little bitches. For this, I had had very few friends. There had only been a few I could understand, being an outcast but, there had been no boy like Damian.

I closed the dark curtain that hung on my window for I didn't want him to see me, especially not the way I had looked just then. Anyone would scream. He hadn't seen me, but I probably shouldn't have been looking out the window anyway. It had not been a wise decision.

The door to my room burst open without a knock. There I saw my brother standing in the doorway. He has broad shoulders and a muscular figure. Every time I looked at him, it left me shocked for I could remember, like it was yesterday, him being the skinniest string bean in the whole world. He wore a grey tank top today and jeans. The tank showed off the "tattoo" of an eye and the freckles that were upon his arms.

"What's with the tank top?" I asked. "It's October."

"Doesn't really matter to me, does it?" he said. "I'm dead anyways."

I rolled my eyes. "What do you want?" I asked.

"I saw who you were looking at, how you were. Don't get close. No one, remember."

I cursed at him, throwing a book in his direction. He catches it with a swift hand before it could hit him. "I told you to stop doing that. It's annoying. Mind your own business, and I wasn't looking at him anyway." It was a lie. "Just, just go away. Now."

"Fine," he said, tossing the book on the bed. "Just warning you. You know what happens."

He walked out of the doorway and went down the stairs, leaving me be. I then went to the bathroom to wash my face. Tomorrow was a day I didn't want to come.

CRYING IN THE RAIN

Damian

The next day had come a lot sooner than I wanted it to. When the bus pulled up to the sidewalk, I had a sickening feeling in my stomach. I had been standing there for a moment, staring at the ground, not wanting to move. The sound of someone clearing her throat came from the bus. As I looked up, I saw it was the bus driver.

"Ya comin' or not? Make up your mind."

I didn't answer her question. I just got onto the bus with anxiety all over me. The door closed and I found my seat. All alone I usually sat. Today was no different than any other day, except that this day, I had noticed the one person I wanted to choke did not get onto the bus. Soon the stress left me. Today might actually be a good day for once if that could happen.

That morning, I had taken my usual seat in English class. Even though I didn't look, I could feel someone's eyes on the back of my head. Ice cold fingertips touched the back of my neck, making me turn suddenly in my seat. There was no one behind me. Everyone else around me who had been working seemed to give me weird looks.

"What a freak," I hear a female voice whisper.

I didn't bother to see who it was. I turn back to my desk feeling stupid. I expected my arch nemesis to jump out of nowhere and stab me in the neck. It wasn't like him to miss a day of torturing me. I had always been watching my back, his words forever ringing in my ears. He said it every time: "Watch your back, little freak, you never know when I might put a stake in it." The bell soon rang, causing me to jump slightly. Laughter escaped some people.

For the final twenty minutes of class, I had been daydreaming. My white lined paper had been blank except for one sentence, "They shall all pay." I grabbed my stuff and left the classroom with Mr. Franklin's suspicious eyes on me. The eyes were always there.

When I had gotten to science class, I sat at my usual table in the lab. Again I was by myself but not for long. Mr. Laurence had just walked into the room when two figures came through the door. The shorter plumplike woman was Mrs. Barns. She had round glasses and gray hair tied in a ponytail. She appeared to be at least in her late sixties but was younger.

Next to Mrs. Barns was the girl. This time I could tell what she looked like for it was day. She had long ginger hair that shined in the light peering through the window. Her skin was very pale, but through the whiteness, you could make out the faintest freckles. Her piercing blue eyes scanned the crowd, wary for she was not used to new faces. She wore black jeans, a studded belt, and an American Horror Story tee shirt. She had several piercings all up her ears. Her nails had been painted black. Everyone else looked upon her with disgust, but if you ask me, I thought she was kind of radiant.

Mr. Laurence whispered something to Mrs. Barns, and she whispered back. He thanked her, and she exited the room, leaving the girl standing there.

"Attention, class," said Mr. Laurence with a polite smile. "This is our new student, Viper Johansson. And… where are you from, Viper?"

"California," said Viper.

The group of girly girls on the right side of the class started to giggle. Perhaps it had been because the girls here were tanner than her. Truth be told, they were fugging orange.

"California," repeated Mr. Laurence. "Quite far indeed. So let's make Viper feel at home, shall we?"

There was no answer. No one had been paying attention expect for me. Mr. Laurence then said, seeing I was the only one looking in his direction and being the only one that was alone, without a partner, "Congratulations, Mr. Winters. You got a new lab partner."

Great. Just great.

Viper didn't talk much. She may have said hi without a smile, but that was it during the class. She kept looking away from me like she was afraid I would start talking to her, which I did during the last five minutes.

"I like your shirt," I commented.

"Thanks," she said as she wrote something down on her observation paper.

I had expected her to be shocked that someone else liked that show too then ask me my favorite season and things of that nature. She didn't though. I guess she found it to be a common thing. I don't know what it was like back in her town or city, but I'm pretty sure it was bigger than here. She probably had friends too with interests like her.

The rest of my day was okay until that afternoon. That was when everything changed. I had been walking to my locker when I see there were pieces of paper taped to my locker. There written in different multiple colors were the words: Emo, Fag, Go Kill Yourself, Suicidal Freak. With an aggravated scream, I tore the papers off my locker. I slipped my stuff into my backpack, slammed the locker furiously, and ran out the building.

Today I walked home, but the commotion caused by the traffic surrounding me did not make the voices in my head disappear. They were back as loud as the night. He had not been there today, but apparently, he wasn't the only one out to get me. Not anymore. They were others. But why did it take them this long to attack? I didn't know.

I'm a freak. A disgrace to everyone, aren't I? Shouldn't I end my life now? If I never give in, it'll just give them what they want.

These were the confusing voices in my head. They were the loss of self-esteem and inner confidence all ramming into each other until I got on my last nerve.

As more thoughts ran through my head, I could feel tears start to stream down my face. Rain then began to fall to the earth as I cried. I pulled my hood over my head, making sure nobody saw me crying. Words ran through my head, causing the urge to creep on me again. The urge to lock myself in my room, to slice my skin until I bled. Crying, I soon found myself running. I kept going faster and faster until I could no longer take the pain inside me. I tripped over my feet, unintentionally making me fall forward and smack my stomach on the cement sidewalk. For a second, I lay there, crying in a puddle until I saw, out of the corner of my eye, a hand outstretched toward me.

Looking up, I saw it was Viper's. As I took her hand, she helped me up from the cement. Through the material of my jeans, I could feel that my knees were bruised from the pain rushing through me as I got up. Once I was up, she spoke to me in a sincere tone, "You okay?"

I didn't answer her. I was thinking about how embarrassed I was that I had fallen right in front of her. I also didn't want to lie. I wasn't okay. Nothing about me was okay, but why would she care? Why would anyone care? Nobody cared about my feelings. Humans were nothing but evil, selfish beings.

"I wouldn't think you were," she said as I looked back up at her from staring at my soggy Converse. "I saw what happened. The papers on your locker. Who put them there?"

"Like you care," I snapped though I didn't mean to.

"Fine, whatever. If you don't want vengeance then see you tomorrow," she said and was about to walk away.

"Wait." I said truthfully, "I didn't mean to snap at you. I'm just kind of angry right now and…"

"Whatever," she said without turning to look at me. "Good night, Winters."

She had called me Winters not Damian. People only called me Winters when they hated me. Great, I had already made another enemy. I had said sorry, but apparently, that wasn't good enough for her. *Whatever! Humans, especially girls, are weird.*

I walked the rest of the way home, which was not far. As I got to the driveway, I noticed something that made me feel about 50 percent worse. The white truck my dad had driven was parked before the house. *He is home. Great.* I wondered what he was going to yell about today.

When I walked in the door, he was standing in the hallway. It made me jump a little, not expecting it. His arms were crossed against his chest. A scowl was on his face that only changed when he talked. "Where were you?"

"At school," I said, it being obvious.

"No shit you were at school, smartass," he said. "What took you so long to get home?"

"I walked."

"That's a long walk," he said, still tense. "Why didn't you just take the bus? Up to no good, are we?"

"No. I just like walking," I said, my eyes scanning the ground.

He didn't say a word. He nodded and walked away from me, which I found odd. I expected something entirely different. Maybe he actually believed me for once or maybe what he had written wasn't one of his moods. *I guess his letter is true.* Why though? Why now after all this time?

That night, we had dinner together for the first time in months. It was steak, nice and bloody like I liked it. The room had been silent for the most part until my father spoke when I was halfway through my dinner.

"How was school?" he had asked.

"Okay, I guess," I lied.

By the look in his eyes, I had gotten mixed messages. One said, "That was good," and another that said, "I don't believe you, you liar." He wiped his mouth with a napkin still staring at me. It was as if he was in deep thought, thinking of what to say. He looked away from me and looked down at his food and some of the tensions flew away from me. He then spoke in a less tense voice.

"Look," he said, glancing up at me, "I know we haven't really gotten along since the incident years ago. I neglected you. I understand that. I know I didn't speak one word to you for quite some years. A couple years ago when you finally became a teenager, I realized what I was missing. But you changed and I did too. I can't...I...I don't know how to relate to you. It's not that I don't love you, but I..."

"Don't bother explaining," I said a little too loudly.

"Damian..."

"Don't," I exclaimed once more.

There was a moment of silence, and I no longer touched the food on my plate. I just sat there staring at it, not sure what to say. Could I believe him after all that had happened? Could we really get along like we used to or would there forever be an unpatched hole in our hearts?

"I know you don't," I said, looking back up. "You don't have to, I'm not going to change. I know you want me to. You said it yourself, but this is who I am. It's not because of her." This made him look up at me. "It's not because of you. It's because of everyone else. It is who I am because I like being this way. And yeah, maybe I'll change a little bit. I will accomplish my dreams that even you say are impossible. I'm not going to waste my whole life being like you. If you wait like this, nothing is going to happen. I would be stuck in this hellhole of a town for the rest of my life if I listened to you. If I did what you are doing, and you know I'm not talking about your so-called career, I would never get to accomplish anything." He looked at me, a little bit offended, as if he did have a heart. "She's dead! Get over it!"

On my last two remarks, the demon inside of me had been unleashed. Not able to even look at him anymore, I got up from my chair and walked to my room. I slammed the door shut behind me and punched the wooden surface. Then I sat on the floor, staring at the space in front of me, my heart racing.

Later that night, I stayed in my room, not wanting to talk to him. I pulled open a notebook and pen from my backpack. Flipping to a blank page, I sat there thinking. I still had not written anything for my English assignment and still could not. It had been an essay, which was something I do not enjoy writing especially this topic. It was "If you had a wish to change something in your life, what would you change and why?" I had a few of those, so not having one wasn't the problem. The problem was the fact that it wasn't any of Mr. Franklin's goddamn business. I supposed he expected stuff like students putting down being rich or becoming famous. In other words, shit that wouldn't happen to them anyway.

What I wanted to say was nothing like that. It was real. My horrible reality. It was something no one experienced in this town because if they went through it, they wouldn't be the way that they are. I knew Mr. Franklin would read this and pull me out of class to talk to me. I didn't need his sympathy, his help. I did not want anyone to. I didn't want to become close personally. I wrote what was true. Why should I deny the past? I didn't want to sound fake. I focused on one night years and years ago.

That night, as I had been writing it, I fell asleep. In my dream, the surroundings of my room changed to that of the past. I was a young boy again, seven years old. I had woken up suddenly from my sleep with the visions of the nightmares in my head. My heart had been pounding in my chest, feeling as though it was going to just leap out onto the floor. Below my stomach, everything was wet, which hadn't been the first time. It was true that I was perhaps too old for this habit, but those nightmares had been too frightening for a boy so young.

Waking up to the darkness had made my fear even worse. Who knew what had been inside of it? The hands of the monsters had slipped through the cracks of the closet door, ready to attack me with a surprising blow. I had run out of the room suddenly, not wanting him to get me. I closed the door behind me, so he couldn't get through. It served him right.

Next, as I had walked down the hallway, I knocked on the door of my parent's bedroom, looking for a safe place to hide from the hairy beast. He might break through any minute now. There was no answer from the other side of the door, so I had knocked once more, only louder this time. Still no answer, no voice inviting me in sounded throughout the air, so I had decided to open the door without permission anyway. Whispering, I had said, "Mom? Dad?"

There had been no answer, and when I had looked into the room, no one had been in there. The bed was still made; its blankets pulled up to the pillows. I had then gotten down the flight of stairs to the kitchen below. No one was there either. The only things that had been moving about were the pans hanging upon the rack above the countertop.

I had run to the living room, checking to see if any human life was there as I began to panic. The room was empty except for the television blaring out some kind of preaching channel. It was as if my mother had disappeared out of nowhere.

"Mom," I had called once more, but still there was no answer.

I had burst through the back door and into the yard. There was the inground pool. Along its sides were lights. There in the pool I could see a figure floating in the water. Around it was a red liquid expanding in the clear water. The figure was my mother, dead.

I had screamed, and a human force had grabbed me from behind. He picked me up in his arms, not wanting me to see this. I didn't understand what had happened as the male figure locked me in my room. I had looked out of my bedroom window after he did. He had been outside, holding my mother in the pool to him. He screamed to the sky, crying. That was the first time I had ever seen my father cry, and ever since that day, it never stopped raining.

DEVIL'S TREE

Slayer

I could smell it in the air. The scent of blood mixed in with the earth around me. As the rust-and-salt sensation traveled up my nose, I looked all around. Soon, upon the ground, I found the tiniest droplet of blood splattered on a crumbled leaf. From that leaf, there was a trail in which I needed to follow. It would lead me closer to unraveling all the secrets. Every step closer I got, the sooner I was to finding this disgrace.

As I followed the trail of red before me, I came to a patch of thorny branches. I pushed them aside so they wouldn't slice into my skin. Freed from them, I came to a giant tree. There was the most horrifying scene I had ever witnessed in all my days. Hanging by a rope tied to a strong branch was a person. In fact, he was a male; his skin had been sliced across his chest as if he had been beaten to death with a chain.

Above the man were more branches with objects tied to them. They had looked like voodoo dolls created with some kind of fabric and sticks. It was a terrible sight indeed, and it just got worse. As I stared at the tree, a crow landed upon one of the braches with a voodoo doll under him.

He eyed me with evil, soulless black eyes. There was a moment of silence until the bird flew off, attacking one of the voodoo dolls. He poked at the eye with his sharp beak. I felt the doll's pain as he did, making me cover my left eye with the palm of my hand. Through the gaps of my fingers, I could feel the warm liquid from inside me escape as it streamed down my hand. Swearing, I ran away, not believing what had just happened.

SAVED

DAMIAN

I woke up the next morning feeling sweaty. At first I thought I had been drowning in the pool, coughing as my eyes opened. Waking up to my dark room, I realized it had been a dream. I wasn't there anymore. That had been the past, but as I came back to where I was, I felt sick to my stomach. I dashed out of my room on that note and went into the bathroom. There I puked my insides out.

An hour passed and the giant yellow transporter to hell had pulled up to the sidewalk. I was even more excited today than yesterday. Not. As I looked up at the windows, one face stood out over the rest. It was Billy Fletcher's. He looked out the window at me, smiling his hateful grimace. His shiny metal-coated teeth just about shined under his sneering lips. As he saw me looking at him, he had made a motion, bringing his hand and swiping it across his throat. Watch out for the knife, little freak, it might be in your throat one day.

"Are you mentally slow," asked the bus driver, "or do you just enjoy staring at nothing but the cars behind you?"

"No."

"Then get your ass on this bus already," she said. I did, and she shut the doors behind me. "There's learning to be done…and you look like you need it."

I ignored her comment and walked down the aisle to get to a seat way in the far end of the bus. I glanced at Billy as I did, and he clenched one fist, smacking it against his other palm. I finally took my seat with the feeling of fear nipping at my neck. When the bus started moving, I knew he was behind me.

"Hey, you little freak," said Billy. I didn't answer. "Hello? I'm talking to you. Are you deaf or something?" I still tried to ignore him, hoping he would go away, but he didn't. "Hey, freak." This time, he yelled it in my ear. "I'm talking to you!"

I turned my head and grasped my ear for a second. He then continued to talk, but this time not directly in the ear. "Glad you can hear. Actually I lied. I don't really give a shit if you can. Did you miss me? Thought I would forget? Oh no, I got people to leave you a message for me. Don't worry. I wouldn't forget. Telling that you're sitting here, I guess you didn't get the idea. Why don't you just die already? Nobody likes you."

I was waiting for somebody to save me, but no one would. Nobody heard him except for two blonde girls, giggling at what they thought was funny. It wasn't a joke to me. What could I say to stand up for myself? What could I do? Why couldn't someone just save me?

Just then the bus doors opened and everyone glanced up but me. I stared down at my feet, as I heard the sound of boot soles hitting the aisle. Soon they stopped and so did Billy. The figure had spoken to him, and as she did, I looked up for I couldn't believe my ears.

"Just shut up, Billy," said Viper. Apparently, she had heard enough of the conversation to know he was torturing me. "No one wants to hear your bullshit."

"What did you say to me?" he asked, getting up from his seat as if challenging her.

"I said shut up."

"Make me," he had said, pushing her on the shoulders, but she barely moved.

Everyone was watching now, but their eyes were not on me. They had been on them. I was surprised the bus driver hadn't done anything to stop what was about to unfold. She was probably too busy texting anyway.

"Gladly," said Viper and, with one fast motion, kicked Billy in the place no boy would wish to be kicked. He collapsed on the ground, cupping the area in pain. Tears came through the corners of his eyes. The whole scene made me laugh for once. In a dry, sarcastic voice, Viper added one more thing, "Have a nice day."

She then took a seat across from me and stared out the window, minding her own business as if nothing had happened. Billy eventually got up. He glanced at me a look as if to say, "She can't save you next time." At the moment, I didn't feel worried though.

I looked back at Viper after that with an uncontrollable smile. I had never seen anyone do that to Billy Fletcher in my life. He deserved it. Eventually, she looked back at me and smiled. Then we began to laugh. Without words, I knew she had forgiven me for snapping at her last night. I liked this human.

Billy hadn't bothered me the rest of the day, which was a good thing. Viper hadn't talked to me at all during science and kept looking down again. I couldn't understand. It was as if she had been too shy to say anything, but then again, she stood up to Billy for me. What was her deal then? I couldn't quite understand. It bothered me more than the eyes on me.

When lunch finally came, I was sitting all alone as usual. I was eating a turkey sandwich, feeling sad at the sight of the empty table. Out of nowhere, a figure sat down across from me. When I looked up, to my surprise, I saw it was Viper.

"Is it all right if I sit here," she asked.

"Yeah," I answered, not feeling so alone anymore.

It was silent for a while except for all the racket everyone else was making. I didn't know what to say or do. My cloak of shyness was enveloping me again. *Why try? She wouldn't want to be friends with you anyway. Nobody wants to be your friend.* I tried to push the voices aside to the point that I blurted out what was on my mind without thinking.

"Do you want to hang out with me sometime? I don't know go to the movies or something?"

"Oh um," she said, confused by the sudden outburst. "I don't know. I mean we shouldn't be friends."

"What do you mean?"

"I mean…Damian. I'm not a nice person. It's best for you if we are not friends."

"I don't understand. You stood up to Billy. How could you not be a good person?"

"I can't tell you," she said quietly as she rose from her seat. "I must go now."

She walked away before I could stand to stop her. I watched her as she ran from the cafeteria, leaving her lunch behind. She was an odd girl indeed, maybe even stranger than I was. I wanted to understand her. I want to know why she thought she was so evil. I wanted to know what she meant or at least change her mind. I wouldn't stop until I did just that.

That night I had gotten home to an empty house except for one little face that was glad to see me, Wolfe. She had been sitting in front of the door (as I walked through the hallway) as if she had known those were my footsteps. Purring, she rubbed the side of her body along my leg as if to say she was happy to see me. I smiled, for animals always made me smile. They couldn't hurt you like humans could.

"Hey, girl," I said, sitting my backpack down on the floor. "Are you hungry?"

On that note, she dashed to the kitchen, fully understanding what I meant.

"Okay, girl," I say as I followed her.

I gave Wolfe her meal, and once more she wagged her tail like a dog. After that, I was about to walk out of the kitchen when I noticed that there was another note on the fridge like before. This time though the message had been different. It read:

Dear Damian,

Meet me at Orville's Pub and Diner tomorrow night at 6:30. Please give me another chance to be your father again.

P.S: I won't be home tonight.

Love, Dad

I pretty much already saw that coming. I guess my father was really sorry. Maybe he really did care. I should at least have given him a second chance to prove that, shouldn't I? I mean he was my father. Still I rolled the message into a cigarette. I had accepted his apology. Maybe.

That night was the first night I dreamt about Viper Johansson. I was sleeping when I felt something cold on my eyelids. It had been the feeling of snow. I opened to see white flakes falling on the ground around me. Lying on its white blanket, I had felt nothing of it. No sudden shock of nipping frost flashed upon me. I felt absolutely nothing, no warmth nor the bitter cold.

The sound of someone calling my voice came from a distance, soon drawing nearer. As I heard this, I got up from the ground slowly. I turned to see a girl coming toward me. It was Viper. She wore a short tattered white dress with specks of blood splattered on it. Blood dripped from her arms and mouth. Her blue eyes looked dark and terrified. In her left hand, she held a dagger. On the dagger's hilt was a red skull and crossbones. The blade was covered in blood. She began to cry in guilt and fear. What had she done?

"We can't be friends, Damian," she said. "I told you. We can't be friends."

I remember, after that scene had faded I woke up to the sight of a bright light before my eyes. A voice spoke, but I didn't know who it was addressing for I was looking at the light.

"You did this. You killed her! You sick bastard! How could you," the voice shouted. It sounded male and seemed familiar. "How could you!"

Suddenly I woke up in my bed. The time was still early, so I fell back to sleep.

SOME THINGS YOU AREN'T MEANT TO HEAR

Mrs. Henderson

I had been sound asleep when the sound of loud shouting woke me. I slowly walked over to the window and peered out from behind the curtain. There across the street was the man of the Johansson household and the girl. They had been standing there on the sidewalk. The man had been shouting something at her, but I couldn't hear. The girl said something back. I also couldn't interpret it.

"Promise me you'll never get in contact with him again! Got it?" yelled the man who was her father.

"I already told you I know," she said.

"Good. We can't blow our cover now," said the father but quieter this time. "Now get in the house."

Viper turned and walked away. The father, on the other hand, looked around the street, causing me to shut the curtain as fast as I could. His eyes lingered at my window. When I heard the car ignition turn, I peered back out, hoping he hadn't seen me. He then drove away. They were suspicious folks all right. What did he mean by "We can't blow our cover now"? Something was up, and I needed to find out what it was.

A NEW BEGINNING

Damian

The next day was a teacher conference day, and I had awoken early not knowing about it. By nine o'clock I had no idea what to do, so I decided to call Miles, seeing I had no friends.

"Hello," answered the other end.

"Hey, Miles. It's Damian."

"Damian," he said excited, him chewing something at the same time. In the background, I could hear metal hitting ceramic, like dropping a spoon in a bowl of cereal. "I'm so glad I finally heard from you. Say, shouldn't you be at school."

"Have the day off."

"So do I, coincidently," he said clearly. His mouth was no longer full. "I've been meaning to talk to you. My cousin Vick. I don't think you know him. He's a year older than you. He goes to a school up in Amberhurst. He's been thinking of putting a band together. Apparently, a lot of people want to be in it surprisingly. He has auditions for it at

Kenny's Music Shop. You know my friend, Kenny. I think you met him before. The tall one with the long hair."

"Yeah, I met him before," I said.

"Anyway, my cousin Vick is going to be the lead guitarist and his friend Fred is the drummer. So we only need a bassist and rhythm guitarist and vocals. Wanna be one of those big bands one day. Do you think you could qualify for any of those?"

"I don't know. I don't play any instruments, and I don't necessarily know if I can sing."

"You shy little chicken shit," mocked Miles. "Stop hiding behind that shell of yours. I know you enough, Damian. Enough to know that inside that passiveness of yours there is a little rebel ready to come out. Just try out, will you? It's not going to hurt."

"I don't know about that. What about me makes you think that?"

"Just shut up, Winters," he said in a friendly manner. "I'm coming to your house in twenty minutes. Look decent."

He hung up, and I knew what he said was true. He would drag me out the door if he had to, to get me there. Miles didn't take anyone's crap.

When he finally arrived at my house, I didn't object, but went with him. We had been in his car when he started talking.

"I used to be like you a lot when I was younger. I was very shy like that. I grew out of it though. You will too eventually. I'm only trying to help you get out of your shell. Don't worry, my cousin doesn't bite... hard," said Miles.

I smiled a little and he did too. There was nothing but silence the rest of the ride.

Soon we arrived at Kenny's Music Shop. There was a line forming outside the door. It was full of people auditioning for the band. If we waited in that line it would take an eternity to get there.

"Holy shit," said Miles seeing all those people. "Good thing I can get you to the front."

"Well, shit," I commented under my breath.

Once we got out of the car, Miles held me by the sleeve of my hoodie as if I was a dog about to run away. He pushed people aside so we could get in. Curse words were thrown at him.

When we got to the front of the line, sitting at table with a bunch of clipboards and papers was a man with long brown hair that was spiky at the top. There were studs below his lips and tattoos covering his chest exposed by the tank top he wore. As soon as he saw me, he stood up.

"Damian, I think you remember the dumb, infamous rock star. The one and only Kenny."

"That is me," said Kenny, holding out his hand. I shook it and he said, "But I'm famous to some people."

"Like who?" asked Miles, "Your friends at the bar?"

"Exactly," he said.

"Well, you may be famous to your bar friends, but you're still an idiot. Look at you, Kenny, it's October and you're still wearing a tank top," said Miles but in a way that friends joke, not meant to insult.

"That is true, but ladies love to see as much of me as they can. Don't they, Maria?" said Kenny, looking at his other employee who had been organizing CDs nearby.

"Eh, you wish," she said cockily.

"Oh someone's feisty," said Kenny and then turned to me. He then opened a red door to his left. "Go on in, little man."

I stood there for a second unmoving until Miles nudged me on the shoulder, telling me to go. I walked through the door, and it shut behind me. I was in a room where they kept their instruments. There in the room were two boys sitting. One of them had been whirling drumsticks around his fingers. The other had been sitting there with his boots on the table. Both of them had been staring right at me.

"Well, you. Tell us your name," said the one who had his feet up on the table with what sounded like an Australian accent.

His glance didn't leave me. He had deep blue eyes, short spiky blond hair, and very pale skin.

"Damian Winters," I said.

The one with the drumsticks wrote this down on a piece of paper. The one with the drumsticks had short brown hair, dark eyes, and olive skin. Both had to be about the same height as me.

"My name is Vick," said the one with his feet upon the table. "This is Fred."

"I know," I said. "Mile's sent me."

"Well, this odda be good," said Vick. "I can tell you are doing vocals since you don't have a guitar with you. So let's hear it. Sing a song for us. Umm…any suggestions, Fred?"

"Sing something Metallica," said Fred.

"Okay," I said and cleared my throat as of getting ready.

I was nervous. I could have run for the door just then. Miles couldn't make me do this, but perhaps he was right. I did sing/scream secretly, but I didn't know if I was any good. I took the shot anyway.

I had nailed it, and by the time I was done singing the song, Vick and Fred had hysterical looks on their face like they had been shocked or brainwashed. Vick was the first one to snap out of his daze, clapping his hands together in applaud.

"Great job. That is what I call singing," said Vick excitedly. "What do think, Fred? Did we finally find our lead singer?"

"When a cat falls from a tree and lands on all four feet," he answered.

"That's just Fred's way of saying welcome to the band." Vick held out his hand, and I shook it. "We'll be the best of friends mate."

That day was when my life finally began to change for the better.

"I told you, didn't I?" said Miles as he was driving me home.

"I didn't know I had it in me," I said.

"Well, you do. I can't wait to see this band together. It's going to be amazing. You doing anything Saturday?"

"Not that I know of," I said.

"Well then, that's you guys first day of practice. I'll pick you up at one. Be ready."

The rest of the day was pretty much boring being home alone. Finally, the sun set early bringing the night time. I walked to the diner my father had told me to go to and was there right on time at six thirty.

Inside the diner was mostly older folk. Those at the bar were yelling at the football game on the TV, angry at their team that was losing. As I scanned the booths, I soon see my father. He had been wearing a tuxedo and had a cheesy smile on his face. I did not smile back but just sat down next to him.

"Hey, kiddo," said my father. "Kiddo" was something he called me when I was little.

"Don't call me that," I said. "I'm not a little kid anymore."

"That is true, Damian," he had said. "I apologize. So is anything new?"

"I'm in a band," I said, staring down at a menu in front of me.

"Really?" he said. "That's really good. Making some friends."

His comment was shocking. I would have expected him to say something like that it would probably be terrible or that there was no point in it for our band would never become famous. He didn't though, and that made me realize that he could have possibly changed.

"How come you're never home?" I asked, which was something that had been on my mind for a while now.

"I'm a business man, Damian," said my father. "Sometimes I have to travel. Sorry if you hate being alone, but I find it a waste of money to have somebody watch you. Besides, isn't it better to do whatever you want?"

"It's not about that," I said. "Some nights you don't come home, and then you're there the next day. I know what you're up to. It's not that hard to figure out."

"And what do you suppose I'm up to?" said my father, raising his eyebrows like he didn't know what I was talking about.

"Why didn't you just tell me," I asked looking up at him, "that there is a woman in your life. Dad, mom's dead. She's been dead for a while now, years. It's okay for you to go out with someone else. I'm fine with it. But for you to keep that a secret is not okay."

"Wow, you finally figured it out," said my father. "I thought you never would. You're a smart boy, Damian. I'm glad you're okay with it too, and I'm sorry I kept it from you. I just didn't want you to think I stopped loving your mother because I didn't. It's time to move on, which was something you made me realize when you stopped moping around. I need to have a life again. So will you meet her one day?"

"Sure," I said.

"I love her, Damian. I've been thinking of marrying her, but I want to know if you like her enough for her to be your stepmother."

"Marriage!" I exclaimed, getting up from my seat. "You're already thinking of marrying her, and I don't even know her."

"Sit down and relax, Damian," ordered my father. "I told you I won't marry her if you don't like her. I haven't even proposed yet. So calm down."

I sat in my seat as he had told me. There was silence between us after that until our food came. "Is that why you asked me to come here?" I asked.

"No," he said. "I was going to tell you about that eventually, but this was for us to bond. It's been a long time since we did that, didn't we? Just give me a chance."

"Fine," I said. "Let's put the past behind us."

THE EYE

Slayer

The doctor had asked me what had happened. I hated lying, but what could I say? I couldn't tell him the truth. That had been extremely confidential just like a lot of secrets in my life. Instead I said that it was a freak hunting accident, which could possibly be true for hunting still had a week left in the season.

"Ouch! You better sue that guy," said the doctor, putting my eye patch on, "Accident or not you need justice."

"You're damn right," I said. "Stupid man mistaking me for a deer."

The doctor chuckled a little and so did I. "Please, I don't mean to laugh at you, just the man's stupidity."

"I understand, sir," I said in my lying act. "I even find it a little humorous too, and I'm the one who had my cornea taken out."

The dumb doctor believed it. With all those degrees, you would expect him to figure out it was a lie. If I had really been shot in the eye, there would have been shrapnel in there, but the human was too stupid to realize that.

When I left the hospital premises, I decided to take a ride down to Stonebrook once more. There I pulled into the driveway of the police station. The police liked me for I had been on their good side. I had always done the right thing.

"Sheriff," I greeted as I walked through the door.

There before me was a lady at a desk, filing information on the computer. She had on a red-and-white striped dress that made her look like a candy cane stripper. She was the sheriff's whore, Lalia. Everyone in a small town like this had to already know; that was why his wife left him. Two-timing scumbag is what he was. As I had walked in, she looked at me and said, "How can I help you, sir?"

"I need to speak to the sheriff," I said. "It is urgent."

"Go on in. I'll call him and let him know that you are here," said the lady.

Walking down the hall, I got to a meeting room where all the cops were having an important discussion. I didn't knock but instead just barged into the room, pushing the double doors so hard, it hit the walls. Everyone looked up at me, hearing the door opening to see who suddenly barged in. The sheriff rose from his seat as he saw me. Everyone else but him stayed quiet.

"My dear old friend," he had said. "What brings you here with such a paniclike demeanor? And mighty god, what happened to your eye?"

"I am here to report a crime. A crime committed by a satanic cult. They are back, and this time they are attacking us."

"No," said the sheriff with absolute worry on his face. "This can't be."

"Oh, but it's true," I said. "Please let me show you."

That night I had brought the sheriff and some of his deputies to the part of the forest that had been blocked off from the hunting range. As the sheriff flashed his flashlight among the tree, his face turned green. I thought he was about to collapse, so I had put a hand on his back to keep him steady. His eyes were full of fear as was everyone else's.

"My god," said the sheriff, "In all my time as a cop, I have never seen something this horrible, this inhumane. They are a lot worse than I had thought. What should we do?"

The sheriff had asked me what to do. The man in charge of this town's safety asked me. He was nothing but a coward and that was shown true. We had to be in over our heads. How a human being could have done something like this is beyond my comprehension. This was not done by no human being but of a bastardly, heartless demon.

CRIMSON

Damian

The next day had come sooner than I wanted it to once more. That morning, Billy had left me alone, but as we got to school, I began to panic. Viper hadn't been on the bus. Maybe she was trying to avoid me and had someone drive her to school. I sure hoped that was the reason because I knew if it wasn't, then bad things would happen to me.

"Looks like your little girlfriend isn't here, does it?" said Billy quietly in my ear as he walked past me in the hall. "You better watch your back, you little freak. You never know when I might put a stake in it."

There were those ear-piercing words again. I tried to avoid him. Maybe he would go away. He did, but before he departed to a different classroom, he stuck his foot out in my path. This made me trip, falling to the tiled ground below. My school supplies flew out of my hands and were flung to the ground with me. Papers fluttered everywhere. My knees ached as I lay there for a second waiting for him to walk away so he wouldn't push me back down if I got up. Soon he did, making me feel safe. No one helped me. No one cared that I was hurt. Why would they? I was just a little freak of nature.

I grabbed my stuff off the ground. Laughter could be heard from people around me (mostly girls). I didn't look at them. I just walked away to my first class with fire on my cheeks. I was so embarrassed.

I thought my horrors were over, but they were just beginning. I was walking to my locker to get my stuff and go home that afternoon when a hand grabbed me by the back of my shirt. It pulled me into the bathroom. A boy with bushy, curly black hair locked the door behind me. The hand that grabbed my back that was Billy's let go.

There they were three of them: Billy, George, and Mike. George and Mike clenched their fists as if to scare me. Billy did the talking.

"So, you little faggot. I've had enough of you. You don't belong here. Time for you to take a swim just like your mother. Pathetic suicidal waste. I don't blame her. If I had a kid like you, I'd kill myself."

My face turned bright red, and I could feel fire in my veins. It was as if steam was about to shoot out of my nose. I turned around fast, throwing my fisted hand at him. He caught it, and pushed me to the ground. George and Mike then grabbed my arms behind my back so I couldn't hit them. They then pulled me into one of the stalls.

Billy lifted the lid of the toilet and said, "Time to drown. Hope it taste pretty in your lungs."

I tried to kick the guys behind me, but as I nailed George in the ankle, he didn't even budge. Billy grabbed onto the back of my head, pulling at my hair. He then brought it forward, and at that point, I was helpless. I took a deep breath before he dunked my head in. I didn't know how long it was, but I was starting to lose my breath when he brought my head up. He then brought it down a second time. They laughed as though my pain was satisfying.

When my head came up the second time, there was a shout of a male voice full of anger. "Shit! We have to run," said Mike.

They did like little wusses leaving me alone finally. I felt dizzy for a minute as I walked over to the paper towels. I dried some of the water from my face, but it didn't help any. I smelled disgusting. The water on my lips poisoned my mouth. When I left the bathroom, all the buses were gone, so it looked like I had to walk home.

That night as I was in the shower, I began to cry. I just wanted it to stop; everything. I want everything to go away. Everyone. Maybe it would be best if I disappeared. Then everyone would be happy with me gone. Their problems solved.

Standing in the fountain of falling droplets, I grabbed a pink razor I saw nearby. It had been hers. She had been in our house when I didn't know, but I didn't seem to care or pay attention to this much. I just took the razor from where the soap was and began to do something I thought I would never do in my life.

Taking the sharp dull blade, I sliced it slowly across the skin of my arm. There was stinging pain as I did this. It felt relaxing. It took the thoughts away as the crimson-colored liquid was exposed through the broken flesh. It trickled down my arm soon to be washed away by the water above. I kept doing this, cutting more and more until I no longer could.

I then sat on the bottom of the tub, crying and licking my wounds. The taste of the salty substance filled my mouth. It was warm and sweet, which was a sick thing to possibly think, but I liked it. I was sick anyway. Wasn't I? My mind was slowly going insane. Rotting, deteriorating from all the words, the voices running through my head. Those evil voices. Oh, how I wish they could go away, but they wouldn't. They never would.

CARVED IN STONE

Damian

The next day, I didn't come to school. I couldn't for they would be waiting for me, yearning to do a lot worse to me. It was as if I was their punching bag. I was as worthless and disgusting as a rat in a subway station to them. I didn't really deserve this. Did I? I couldn't be that pathetic, could I?

That morning when I woke up, I ran my finger over the scratches that I had inflicted upon myself. *How could I have done this?* I think and then get up from my bed.

As I went downstairs, I gave Wolfe food like I did every morning. As I refilled her water bowl and the cold liquid fell, that night flashed in my eyes again. Wolfe meowed after a moment, snapping me back to normal.

"I'm fine, girl," I said, setting the bowl on the floor.

The way she looked at me with those beady eyes, it was as if she had known something was wrong. She could sense I was in pain. I could have just been imagining things, but I wasn't. She licked my hand in a sympathizing manner. Then she began drinking some of her water. Who said a cat couldn't be man's best friend?

After I had gotten dressed, I decided to take a walk. Everyone would be in school by then, so the buses wouldn't have seen me, wondering why I wasn't at school. I said good-bye to Wolfe then walked out the door.

The air was cold and quite breezy just like I liked it. I usually hated the feeling of sleeves on my arms, but this time, I left them down to cover my cuts. I didn't want anyone to know what happened. Then they would ask me all kinds of questions I didn't want to answer.

Soon I had been walking past Kyle's Coffee Shop when I saw a florist shop. Walking in, the first thing I saw was a person. A short, petite woman with short blond hair worn in a bob was watering tulips. She wore blue jeans, a green tee shirt, and an apron. As the bell above the door chimed, she looked at me.

"How can I help you," she asked.

"I'd like to buy a bouquet of red roses," I said.

After I had bought the roses, I took a trip to the cemetery. There I placed the flowers in front of a headstone that read,

Mrs. Marie Winters
October 24, 1968–September 2, 2000
Rest in peace

As I laid them on the green grass, I heard the sound of footsteps behind me. I turned my head and saw Viper. *What is she doing here?*

"Was she your mother?" she asked. I didn't answer her. She shouldn't have been here. Yet she continued to speak, "I understand what you feel. My mother is dead too."

I didn't expect that comment from her. I knew I had never seen her mother before, but I had never thought that she had lost hers too. I hadn't really thought anything of it. If I did, my first thought would have been divorce. Wasn't that everyone's first thought?

"I'm sorry," I said, which I never understood why we say it, sorry.

"Don't apologize for something that is not your fault. I hate that," she said. "If it is sympathy you are trying to give me, don't give me that either. I don't need it."

She was from a strong bunch, wasn't she? I have never met a girl like her in my life before. You could hear it in her voice when she spoke that she had been through a lot, but she wouldn't ever stand down from the obstacles in front of her. The girls I knew crumble to the ground in tears if they broke a nail. Viper, on the other hand, did not even show the slightest bit of tears as she talked about her mother's death.

"I never met her. She died when I was a baby. I was almost two years, my brother almost a year." *I didn't know she has a brother. Why haven't I seen him before?* "From what I heard from my dad, she was murdered. The police never found out who killed her. Her name was Clare. Clare Johansson. It must be worse for you, having known your mother."

"How did you know that?" I asked.

"Math," she answered, "You were seven years old on September 2, 2000."

"What are you doing here?" I asked, changing the subject.

"I come and go as I please. I have been quite ill lately. That is why I was out yesterday."

"Not that. Why are ya here talking to me? Last time I talked to you, you said you couldn't be my friend. You said you were a bad person and then you ran away."

"I like you, Damian," she said, as though it hurt her to say it. "I wish I could be friends with you, but I can't."

"Why?" I got up from kneeling upon the ground, a little angry now. "Why do you think you're so bad? You're perfectly fine to me."

"I'm different than everyone else, Damian," she said, doing that thing where she looks away from me.

"So am I."

"I'm different than you too," she said. "It just wouldn't work. Once you found out the truth, you wouldn't want to be my friend anymore. They always leave. Bad things happen to them after that."

I realized this girl was as delusional and messed up in the head as I was. She didn't feel like she belonged. I tried being her friend many times during science, lunch, and now. I still got the same answer. It was like trying to pry open a box covered by a thousand locked chains sunk at the bottom of the ocean with man-eating sharks swimming around you or at least something like that. She was as hard to read as Morse code.

"I won't," I said. "I don't have any friends. Please, just one day. Hangout with me, and maybe you'll change your mind."

"Fine," she said, giving in.

"Saturday night. The movies. Your pick."

"Okay," she said. "But let's get this straight. This isn't a date."

"Of course not," I said, the vision of her kicking Billy in my mind. "I owe you anyways."

ACQUAINTED WITH SATAN

LALIA

I had been walking down the street one night. The sound of my pumps hitting the cobblestone pathway rang in my ears. As I was walking, I had the feeling that somebody was following me, so I whirled around. There was nobody there. I then began to walk again, but then I heard it. The sound of someone else's footsteps was behind me once more. I turned, and once more saw no one, but the sound still followed.

It was as if I was being chased by a ghost. I halted where I was, causing the sound to stop. I thought for a second, *Maybe it is my shoes.* I slipped the heels off my feet and went on. The cold stone ground rubbed against my feet. The sound still sounded though, causing me to ask out in the darkness, "Who is there?"

There was no answer. The sound was of the wind rustling what was left of the leaves on the trees nearby. I turned back and walked forward. I had to get back to my apartment soon before I froze my ass off. Nearing the corner of the brick building, I felt a hand grab me. It covered my mouth to stop anyone from hearing my screams. After that, everything went black.

Eventually, I was awakened by the shaking movement all around me. I had to be in a van or truck of some sort. As my eyes opened, I saw nothing but the darkness of a blindfold. My hands were tied behind my back with rope, as were my feet.

Soon the shaking stopped. The sounds of the turning of a key in the ignition, the opening of a door, and footsteps on a concrete road were all heard. Another door was opened and a person climbed up.

"What do you want from me?" I asked, crying. "Is this Mrs. Harrison? I'm so sorry for sleeping with your husband. Please, don't kill me."

"Shut up," said the voice, which could only be male. Using his hand, he smacked me across the face hard, leaving a sharp, tingling pain upon my cheek.

"Please, sir, let me go," I said, pleading. "I'll do anything you want just please don't hurt me."

He didn't say anything. Instead he covered my nose and mouth with a rag that smelled of chemicals. As I could no longer breathe, my face smacked to the bottom of the van as I passed out.

When I woke up again, I found myself in a standing position. My wrists and ankles were chained to the walls by shackles, which I could feel were causing me to bleed. I had been in and out of consciousness constantly, not knowing where I was. All I remembered was wanting to get out.

Around me the walls were covered in other victim's blood. It ran through the crack and crevices of the concrete, pouring down to the floor below. It was fresh, maybe it had been there a day but was never longer than that. He was obsessed with this slaughter, for these gallons of blood could not have been taken from one person only. I knew from this point I wasn't going to make it out alive.

Before me was a giant room, a basement to be exact. There in the room were tables, and behind that were shelves upon the walls. Jars with animal parts and human ones inside them hung upon the shelves. Weapons and books lay on the tables. Some were covered in blood, for he reused those weapons every time.

Just then, as my eyes had met something I didn't want to see, I heard the door open. Heavy footsteps of a muscular man coming down the metal staircase were heard accompanied by the echo of a ringing sound. He wore a black cloak with a hood that covered his face for he didn't want me to see him, maybe even to recognize him.

"You're awake," he said and took a giant butcher knife covered with blood off the table.

I wanted to scream through the fabric covering my mouth, but he had not hit me with it. Instead he took a rag hanging by the end of the stair railing and swiped the blade clean of blood. He then put it down and picked up a smaller knife from the table. As he walked over to me, my heart beat fearfully in my chest, and I fell out of consciousness again.

PLEASE TELL ME

Damian

Saturday soon came, and Miles picked me up in his car once more; but this time, it was to drive me to his cousin's house up in Amberhurst. There we were to practice in his garage or something like that.

"Have a nice couple of days?" asked Miles as he looked out to the road in front of him.

"It was okay," I said, telling a repetitive lie, which I had been good at doing. "What can I tell ya? It's school. How about you?"

Miles chuckled before he spoke. "I used to say that when I was your age. Probably told ya this before, but I hated school until now. College is nothing but partying after working. Kind of like the rock star life."

A minute passed, and as we turned onto the highway, the sun flashed into my eyes suddenly. I squinted as I pulled the visor down. Doing this caused the sleeve of my hoodie to fall down, exposing my cuts. Miles must have seen this for he made a gasping sound.

A few seconds of silence went by as if he was trying to find the words to say. What he did say, I didn't expect, "I used to do the same thing ya doin'. I was bullied a lot growing up. I didn't say anything. I just kinda kept it to myself. My parents barely had time for me, time to notice what was wrong. And my sister was dying. It felt like there was no light, but there was, there is. Damian, if there is something so bad that is making you do this then I want to help you. I want you to know, I'll always be your friend even when no one is there for you. I'll always be there."

I didn't know whether to cry or smile. He actually wanted to be my friend. I hadn't had anyone say something like he did before, and I really didn't know what to say to it.

"What happened, Damian?" he asked. "Please tell me."

"I'm sorry. I can't," I answered, not wanting to tell him. I barely even knew him.

"Why not?"

"Because I can't," I said.

"Fine. When you're ready, tell me," he said. "I'm not going to make you tell me anything. Just to let you know if you don't tell anyone, things will just get worse."

There was complete silence between us after that until we got to Vick's house. Then he got out of the car, a giant smile on his face as if nothing had ever even happened, as if the conversation we had didn't ever take place. My secret was kept.

"Hey, Vick," he said as I had closed the car door.

Looking up, I saw Vick walking down the steps toward us. "Aye, guys," said British Vick. "Come on in. My mum's a gotten the lunch ready. Hope you like pizza. How about you, Damian? You ready to write some song lyrics soon?"

"Sure, I guess," I said kind of shyly.

"All right now let's get me some pizza," he said, holding open the door for us. "Ladies first." He motioned to Miles, who wacked him in response playfully on the head as he walked by.

THE DEMONIC EYES

In Vick's house, everything was so bright inside and clean. Much cleaner than my house at the moment for everything was so polished so squeaky clean that the windows seemed to shine like crystals in the beating sunlight. The wooden floor was so spotless that I was afraid to step on it and possibly leaving dirty tracks behind. I thought to take my sneakers off, but Vick didn't, neither did Miles, so I didn't bother too.

Walking first through the door, a staircase lay to the northwest and near it was an opening in the wall leading to their family living room. To my right was another opening like the other, but this led to their dining area. Behind the entryways, I could tell there were mahogany double doors folded behind the walkway. The house was quite nice and felt welcoming in a way, which eased the shyness in me. There was nothing to be afraid of. These people had to be friendly. If they weren't, why would Miles like them?

"This way," said Vick, escorting us around the house as if he was a tour guide. He was definitely a different kind of kid. There was a bit of an actor's attitude within him. "Now as we walk down the corridor, you will see food pantries to your left and right. Please do not touch even if it kills you, Miles." He looked to Miles. Miles laughed at Vick's weird butlerish accent. Vick continued, "And this way, we shall continue our tour to the kitchen where this lady stands there placing pizza upon paper plates. Yet she has an extravagant kitchen, she does not wish to cook. Or at least we don't want her too."

The kitchen we had entered was quite extravagant and far bigger than our kitchen. It reminded me of the one I had once seen long ago in a house that is nothing but a memory. Pans hung from a rack in the middle of the room, dangling above the countertop high above where the woman had been placing plates. The countertops were white marble with gray specks scattered about it, and upon the floor were white tiles. I could have sworn it was the same kitchen.

As the woman turned around slowly at the sound of Vick's voice, she did not stumble in her ridiculously long black heels. As her blue eyes met mine, a vision flashed within me. For a second I thought she was my mother dressed for her day to work. Today she wore black heels, a black skirt, and a red-and-white polka-dotted blouse. Her long brown hair had been straightened. A smile lit her face as she saw me. As she said my name though, I came back to reality. The woman wasn't the same anymore. My mother's brown hair disappeared and turned into blond, her face for someone else's, but the figure was just as svelte. She wasn't my mother but Vick's mother.

"How great it is to finally meet you," she said, coming toward me with an outstretched hand. I shook it in courtesy, and she began to ramble on, "Vick and Fred have been talking all about you. They have been explaining to the others, 'The new vocalist you should hear him. He's is just so amazing. We are going to be the next greatest band.' I haven't seen Vick and him so excited for anything. That and when Vick got to be in his Uncle Jim's new horror movie he produced. I don't know if you heard of it, but it is his first movie. In theaters this weekend…"

"Ma," said Vick, patting her on the back, "he gets it."

"I'm sorry," she said, not realizing that she had still been shaking my hand as she rambled on. She let go, and I was starting to think she may have had one too many. "It's been a long time though since Vick has been so happy, since he made new friends. It just makes me feel so relieved. Been some tough years."

"What is the name of the movie?" I asked, it sounding familiar.

"*The Ax Murder in the Forest*," she answered. "Supposed to be a good one, but I can't stand horror movies. But since it's Jim's and Vick is in it, I guess I'll have to watch it. You'll have to meet Jim; he is supposed to come over soon anyway. He wants to see this new band."

"Mum, for the last time, his name is Jimbalya," commented Vick in a regular New England accent. He had already taken a bite of his pizza.

"Vick St. Fernandez, you have no hospitality. Will you wait 'til everyone is sitting down? And you go in the kitchen with that."

"Fine," said Vick with a stuffed face, walking away.

"Why do they call him Jimbalya?" I asked, finding it a weird nickname. "Does he like rice or something?"

"No, you silly goose," she said with a weird fake laugh.

"We call him Jimbalya because when I was a baby I used to call him that instead of Jimala, and it just kinda stuck," said Vick, walking back in the room. "Come on. I'll introduce you to the rest of the band and then we'll have lunch."

He walked to a door, and I followed him to the garage. Inside three other people were setting up instruments. Toward the back of the room was Fred's drum set ready go. He was there leaning against the wall practically asleep. One guy, who had been tuning his guitar, stood closest to us. He had a full-out spiky Mohawk dyed a bright red. He had some tattoos on his arms and small black gauges, kind of like how Miles's had been. Even though he had that print upon his skin, I knew he couldn't be much older than me. The other kid had been leaning over to plug her bass into the amplifier, which caught my eye.

As we walked through the door from the hall that connects the kitchen to the garage, their eyes looked up at me. The girl plugging in the bass jumped from the unexpected noise before she looked up. Her green eyes looked into mine as she had glanced over. She had long straight black hair with pink ends. She was average in height and quite skinny. When I saw her, I began to like this band idea a lot more.

"Hey, guys," said Vick, jumping down the steps. "This is Damian. Damian this is Ace and Roxxi. They're brother and sister. Ace is sixteen. Roxxi is fifteen."

As he said this, I began to see some resemblance. "What's up," I said, trying to be friendly and act cool.

"The ceiling," answered Ace, pointing upward.

I smirked and then there was a moment of awkward silence; nobody knowing what to say next.

"Hellooo," asked Mrs. St. Fernandez, "there is food in the dining room."

"Food," exclaimed Fred and Vick, running past her more for the thought of attempting to be funny rather than being extremely hungry.

The others followed, and I was the last one to walk up the steps of the garage. I didn't feel that hungry at all. Perhaps it had been that I was nervous, shy of meeting these people I have never met before. Why should I have been? I do not know. Or maybe there were still thoughts in my head of Miles's conversation in the car. I still couldn't get over the fact of someone else knowing my wrong whether or not they had done it once themselves. As this crept in my mind, I could feel my wounds burning slightly.

"So, Damian," asked Vick, after swallowing a bite of pizza, "have you ever had singing lessons?"

"No," I answered truthfully.

"Well, blimey," commented Vick in a British accent, practicing his acting once more. "That is quite impressive. You sing so well."

"Thank god," said Fred, pointing his thumb at Vick. "We wouldn't want this guy singing. We'd turn into Broadway."

"Hurtful," said Vick, coming back in his normal voice, "but true. I can't scream for my life except of course in horror movies, but that is different."

After the plates were cleared, we came to our real first band discussion.

"So what should we name this band?" asked Vick, which had been a good point. Every band needed to start with a name. "I was thinking something a little metally."

"Metally?" asked Fred, laughing at his lack of knowledge in English.

"Oh shut up. You know what I mean," said Vick, "So does anyone have ideas?"

"How about the…," started Roxxi thinking, "The Bloody Marys."

"No," disagreed Ace, shaking his head. "I mean it's a good name, but it just doesn't fit. After all, there is only one girl. One Bloody Mary."

"I was talking about the drink, stupid," said Roxxi. "Like you got anything better off the top of your head."

"Who's to say I do or don't," commented Ace, bickering with her. "If you gonna name a band after a drink, you might as well call it Drinks on the House. Then everyone will come to our gigs."

This had made me and the others chuckle a little except for Roxxi, who looked a little red in the face from her defeat.

"Fred," asked Vick, "you got any?"

"Yeah. The Rise of the Phoenix."

Vick nodded his head while biting his lips as if thinking it over. "I like that. How about you Damian? Do you have anything?"

I sat there for a moment, looking at every one of their faces, puzzling it over, wondering if what I was about to suggest would be lame. "How about…The Demonic Eyes."

"The Demonic Eyes," repeated Ace to himself, mumbling, as if trying to figure if it sounded right.

"I like that one as well," nodded Vick. "We could wear fake contacts to make our eyes all demonic. What about everyone else? You're all abnormally quiet."

"I like it. The ideas also good."

"Same," said Fred, and the others nodded, agreeing.

"Then how do we settle this," Vick had wondered.

Ace reached down to take something out of his pocket. He tossed a silver quarter onto the table then slapped his hand down on top of it to stop it from rolling. "Heads…The Rise of the Phoenix, tails…The Demonic Eyes. Agreed?"

We agreed. Ace flipped the coin into the air with the flick of his thumb. It then landed on his other hand. He immediately cupped it, not wanting the object to go flying onto the floor. When he pulled it back he said to us, "Tails."

"Sold! And it goes to Damian Winters with The Demonic Eyes," exclaimed Vick, pointing his index finger at me as if he was an auctioneer.

So there we were with a name, and thinking about it, it wasn't that bad. At first I thought the name wasn't that great, but I came to change my mind. The rest of the day, we pretty much started talking about songs and stuff. I was to write lyrics for one by the end of the week. I didn't really know how, but I had to try my best. Everyone was counting on me.

I wasn't really sure how this whole band thing worked. Sure, I listened to a lot of them, old and new of different subgenres, and I knew of what rock life was about. What I didn't know was how exactly to write the music. What words could I say? Whatever. That was something to think about later not now.

"Good-bye," waved Vick later that afternoon from the porch steps.

I waved back and then got into Miles's car, ready for another long one-hour drive back to home. There had been so much on my mind that I had almost forgotten about the date with Viper. Well, it hadn't been a date as far as she was concerned. I didn't know what exactly that was, but I guess I could admit that I was starting to fall for Viper Johansson secretly. Never have I done that before.

"Well, that went well. Yes?" asked Miles was he drove down the highway. It began to rain heavily that we could barely see anything on the road even with the windshield wipers on. "They seem to like you."

"Yeah," I said. "They're very nice."

There was a moment of silence, and then Miles brought up what I didn't want to talk about once more. "About what happened earlier. You need to tell me what's wrong. If you did that to yourself there obviously is a reason."

"I…I barely even know you, Miles," I said, not wanting to explain my life to him. "Why do you even care? You shouldn't. No one does."

"I care about you. It doesn't matter if others don't 'cause that isn't going to change the fact that I care about you," he said, looking back at me every now and then from the pouring rain. "I care because you're my friend, Damian. Sure, I don't know you as well as other friends know each other, that's for sure, but that's because you've always been just an accomplice until now. Besides, you're not exactly letting me be your friend right now. Friends know everything about each other and keep their secrets to the grave.

"I wasn't lying to you, and I don't want it to sound as if I am yelling at you. I'm not. I'm telling you what is fact. I used to do the same thing you're doing when I was depressed as hell. There are many reasons why, and I'm sure you have reasons to, but it doesn't make it right. It doesn't change anything, Damian. Those reasons, they're never put to peace until you say something. I sure did, and look at me now. Life certainly got better for me. They can for you too. What you feel inside will only get worse if you don't tell someone, and I know you have no one else to tell."

Feeling pathetic and weak inside, I began to cry. My eyes watered then the tears began to stream down my face. I tried to hold them back, not to let him see me crying, but they were clogging my throat. I would croak when I spoke, revealing that I was feeling emotional. I looked out the window, away from him.

"You wouldn't understand me," I responded, a crackle in my voice. "Or...maybe you could but there are things I can't tell you. I can't. Don't make this any harder than this already is."

Mile's voice changed tone, softer now, almost a whisper, putting a hand on my shoulder. "Hey, it's okay. I'm sorry." I didn't speak nor turn my head to see him. "I'm sorry."

I nodded it off and thanked him for the ride when he pulled up to my house.

"No prob. I'll see ya next Sat. Right?" he asked as I opened the car door.

"Yeah," I confirmed and shut it behind me.

THE HOUSE

Damian

That night, the rain had finally stopped; and when it did, I finally remembered what I had not long before.

"Shit," I cursed.

At the sound of the word escaping my mouth, Wolfe jumped as if she had known it had been bad. I chuckled a little bit and searched for Miles's number. When I found it, I dialed to hear him say hello. I hung up immediately after that. Was I that stupid that I had forgotten what had happened thirty minutes after it had occurred? I couldn't call him up asking for a ride. Sure, I had no other way of getting there by car, but I couldn't make him angrier then I probably did. I didn't want to tell him the truth either, and that was the only way I was going to get around this one. I had to walk with Viper to the movie theater, no question in thought.

"What are you doing here?" asked Viper as I begun to walk up the steps of the scary old mansion.

"We were…"

"I know that," she said before I could finish as she closed the door behind her. On the top step of the porch, she said, "I mean what are you doing at my house? I was just about to walk to yours."

She seemed to be almost scowling at me. "Umm…What is wrong with me walking to your house?"

"'Cause you shouldn't be near this house. Come on. Let's go before anyone sees you."

"Why?" I asked as she took me by the arm, practically dragging me as she ran.

"I told you," she started, and as she went past my house, she stopped running and let me go, "we're not supposed to be friends, but if you must bring me to this movie then bring me."

"Okay," I said, shrugging off the whole episode for I know I would only get some weird, hazy, vague, and confusing response. I figured all girls were weird anyway and left it at that. "Let's go then."

We walked to the movies without her questioning why we had walked. That walk had been nothing but silent. When we had got to the theater, we both had agreed to see *The Ax Murder in the Forest*. She had seemed to be the type that would watch horror movies, so I hadn't been surprised when she said yes. Any other girl I would have. She seemed to talk to me with a straight, bored expression on her face. There was not even the slightest smile. Nothing. Maybe she had hated me after all and really didn't want to be my friend. She was hard to decipher.

I had bought us popcorn and some candy. She had thanked me as we walked to the theater.

"You're welcome," I replied and opened the door for her.

There had been so much blood and gore in that movie. I couldn't believe Viper was sitting there so normally. She didn't scream, lean into my shoulder, or cover her eyes from the horrid sight. Instead as I had looked over at her, a smile was spread across her face. This had my lips spread across my face as well. She had a nice smile, so pure and white.

Vick had died when the murderer sliced his throat open with an ax. His head slid off his body, spraying blood everywhere. For some reason, I found it hilarious to see someone I know being killed in a horror film. I started to laugh uncontrollably. Everyone around me turned to look at me, glaring a "what the hell is wrong with you" glance.

When I stopped, I noticed Viper was looking at me the same way and I blushed, pink splotches hit my cheeks. She probably thought I was some kind of messed-up psycho. She finally asked after about a minute, "How was that funny?"

"I know that guy."

"Sure you do," she said, sarcastic.

"Seriously," I answered. "We're in a band."

"Really," she said, seeming to lighten up.

"Yeah," I said. "I'll tell you about it later."

After the movie, Viper walked beside me when she brought up the conversation we had started before.

"So you are in a band?" she had asked.

The moon was far above our heads. Its light shined down on her beautiful face, and I couldn't help but blush once more. I tried to hide it, scratching my neck for a second nervously. I wasn't sure why I was nervous though. "Yeah. We just started it. We haven't written any songs yet though."

"What's it called?" asked Viper looking up at me, a sparkle in her glittering blue eyes.

"The Demonic Eyes."

"Well, cool. What kind of band are you? Have you decided?"

"A metal band," I answered.

"Really? That's awesome," she said with a smile. "I love metal. So what are you?"

"Vocals," I answered, and she seemed surprised.

"I didn't know you sang."

"Yeah. I can," I answered, for the first time vehemently proud.

Viper had been acting like a totally different person. One minute she had been saying she didn't want to be my friend, but near the end of the movie, she seemed to be enjoying herself. I had as well forgotten my fears of everything else around me. I felt important. As I talked about myself, Viper nodded and looked at me, holding on to everything I was saying.

THE DEMONIC EYES

We stopped walking when we got to my steps. I knew she hadn't wanted me guiding her to her house down the dark dirt path. Why so? There was something about that house that had seemed to frighten them, especially the old woman across the street. I wasn't sure what it had been, but I wanted to know. I was becoming more and more curious.

"Well, thank you," she said, which had shocked me a little. "I actually had fun."

"You're welcome," I said.

She walked a little closer then began to lean into me. I couldn't believe it, but she was in fact about to kiss me. I closed my eyes as her lips touched mine, gentle and soft. As they locked, butterflies began to flap around in my stomach. I could feel my cheeks growing red.

When we stopped, she said, "Good night, Damian."

She then walked away calm, cool, and collected, without another word to say. I watched her as she walked down the long path to her house until I could no longer see her figure in the dark.

I walked into my house and collapsed onto my bed. So many thoughts went through my head, but these voices were joyful. *She actually kissed me! Does that mean she likes me? Will she be my friend now or, even better, my girlfriend? What does it mean? Oh gosh, shut up! You sound like a girl.*

I fell asleep with Wolfe lying above my head, purring. That night I had another dream.

There on the ground, I awoke to the feeling of fingers running through my hair; and as my eyes opened, I saw Viper there beside me. Her ginger hair was now a dark black; her blue eyes consumed me. I couldn't believe that she had been this close to me. Her red lips not far from me; I could feel her breath escape her, skimming my lips.

As we lay on the blanket of snow, I felt nothing. There was not the feeling of warmth or bitter cold. All I felt was numb all over, but my heart still beat, beating faster with her beside me. I parted my lips to speak, to question. She put an index finger to my lips, silencing me.

Grasping palm to palm, entwining fingers with mine, she lifted me from the ground. Then she brought me to the path, and we ventured down the trail. The sunlight dimmed and dimmed to the point; when we arrived at our destination, night had fallen. No light in sight.

At first I couldn't see anything. My feet were planted on the ground, not knowing my surroundings. Then a light went on, a light in the window of the house, the house we've been grown to fear. In the window a figure stood. A woman dressed in white, hair tied back. On her face was a terrifying smile, her eyes never blinking, stared at me.

Another window was visible as another light came on. In it a man stood. He was old, hair of white, skin of grey. He too stared just the same. After him, soon more dim lights came.

When the house was full, they started coming toward us from the forest, closer and closer. I wanted to say something to Viper, but I remembered she silenced me. And as I realized this, my lips seemed to have been pasted shut. I was unable to move them the harder I tried. I squeezed her hand so tight, but she didn't budge. The sleepwalkers came closer, drawing nearer. My only way out was to leave Viper for she wouldn't help.

Yanking my hand from her, I kept my eye on the sleepwalkers. Her grip tightened as I tried to squirm away. I then glance at her to see a row of sharp fangs, blood dripping down her face. Frightened, I yank with all my might. Her hand crumbled like that of plaster then the rest of her crumpled to the ground in a pile of dust.

That was when I started running. With heavy breathing, I headed toward the path, but I was stopped. A ring of the sleepwalkers surrounded me, blood dripping from their face. I fell, sunk to the grass as a sky full of arms suffocated me.

MORE BLOOD

Slayer

A young man found another one that week. He had been walking through the woods to find the river in hopes of going fishing. On his way, he found a woman, naked, sliced in half on the forest floor. A symbol of an eye was carved into her stomach.

I know it was the police's job to handle this, but what did they know? They couldn't handle the situation. Just little townies not the big shits. I was doing them a favor stepping in. Besides, I had business involved.

"It was Lalia," said the sheriff. He was holding back the urge to cry. "What could I have done?"

How about not cheating on your wife?

"There was nothing you could have done," I assured him. "None of us saw this coming."

"I can't handle this, dear friend." There was a quiver in his voice. "What's to do?"

"We need to call the FBI," was my only answer. And so we did.

WE ARE WATCHING YOU

Damian

Body consumed by the horrors of my nightmare, I had awoken in fright. The visions of that house were still within my mind. My dream had to mean something. With all the rumors about that place, there had to be something strange that went on. What was the big secret?

The dream had seemed so real. It took me all day to shake it off. I wanted to know the truth. I had to know, and I knew just the place to find out.

Mrs. Shoster stared me down as I entered the library. She was always a grumpy broad.

I walked passed her, returning the frown, to the archives. First I looked through the newspapers, but I wasn't sure what date to look for. I searched the computers, typing in the address of the house.

"'The Newman house sold today.' Article written by Clarence Jones."

It had just been an article about the Johanssons. Useless.

"Newman house burned down. 1871."

Now we were getting somewhere. Apparently the house had been burned down after some strange events. They didn't clarify what the events were but there was a mention of a disappearance.

"...right after Rose Newman's disappearance."

I then searched for the disappearance of Rose but still nothing came up, so I went back to the Newman house adding 1900s.

"'Newman house on fire.' 1935."

Another fire? I clicked on the link, getting only to the end of the first paragraph when pixels began to dance across the screen. The entire screen was then covered in snow. Within the snowy pixels words came across the screen written in red. "We are watching you."

As I looked at the words, the red text began to transform into liquid coming out of the computer screen. It streamed down the table, covering the desk and my hands with the crimson.

My heart began to race, growing louder and louder until I could feel it in my ears. My skin felt as if I was burning as my breath began to stagger. I had to have been going into a panic attack.

I looked up from my hands as I hear the clearing of a throat. There I see on a computer across from me a man. "Are you all right?"

Glancing down at my hands, I saw nothing but pale clean skin. Then looking to the computer screen, there was nothing but the desktop background. There had been no blood, no words. "I'm fine," I muttered to the man, not believing what had just happened if it even did.

By the time I went back onto the Internet, my time logged out. I sat there a few minutes just staring at the main log in screen. No thoughts wavered within my head of the phenomenon that had just taken place. I was too confused and too tired to question.

Being a bit far, I had taken my bike to the library, which I mounted upon after my odd experience and was about to return home. Halfway there, my cell phone rang.

"Hello?" I asked.

"Hello, Damian," said an eerie voice. I knew it couldn't be anyone I knew. Maybe it was just Billy and one of his tricks, but it couldn't be. It sounded nothing like him.

"Who is this?"

"The man with the scar," he said then after a long breath, he added, "I'm going to get you, boy, and your friend too."

With that there was a click and the line was dead. I stood there for a few seconds then tucked the phone in my pocket. *So you are telling me that (1) the whole occurrence in the library happened, and (2) I get this crazy call from a guy who wants to get me and my friend?* Perhaps there was something even more wrong with me than I was aware of, or maybe it had just been a prank. Yes, a prank. I wasn't crazy. It was just some idiotic fools out to get me.

That night, after hours of trying to fall asleep, I dreamt. I had been filling up a car with gas. I have no idea where the car had come from. I didn't have a car.

The night was dark and chillier than usual. I zipped my jacket in hope of keeping more warmth, but it didn't help much. I jumped slightly on my toes. My breath could be seen before me in a plume of fog. As I glanced around me, pump in hand, I saw only an empty road. The only lights were from the gas station and my headlights.

I was about done pumping the gas when I saw a figure. Though it was dark, he appeared very clearly to me from the flashing of the gas station's podium lights. He had the same aura as the man in my dream except this wasn't him. I knew for there was something in his voice that sounded familiar. The man on the phone.

He wore dark jeans and a black muscle shirt with a hood. Through the sleeve of his shirt, a large, deep cut, a scar the length of his torso could be seen. With half a sneer, he held up his hand, two fingers clasps. From those fingers are my car keys, dangling.

"Hey," I yelled, putting my pump back, my eyes still fixed on the man. "Those are my keys!" Still standing there, the keys dangled in the scarred man's hand. "What do you want?" No response. "I said what do you want?"

Before my eyes, he disappeared and my fingers went to my pockets, looking for the keys there. Just as I reached into the empty pocket, I felt an arm grasp around my waist, a knife at my throat. "I got you now and your friend's next."

The blade slashed through me. First there was the burning then I was choking on my blood.

I had awoken not much later, screaming, my eyes wide open. A bright light flashed before my eyes. In the light soon a shadow of a figure came toward me. I could hear his voice but not see him.

"It's okay," he said. "There is nothing wrong. Calm down. Just calm down."

At the sound of my father's voice, my screaming ceased. "Go back to sleep."

And so I did.

THE PLEASURE OF THE CRIMSON DRINK

Anonymous

I had been running. The puddles of the falling rain splashed beneath my boot soles. I had it in my backpack, safe and secure, so being caught wasn't the reason I had been running. I had seen something in the woods. I had seen him. He was coming for us again, and to think we had enough enemies.

I kept looking behind me, thinking he was there. He wasn't so I slowed. I was shaking as I walked, and I could feel my veins go empty. My head began to swirl, a black rose beginning to bloom in my vision.

Starting to run again, I headed to an alleyway between two stores. There was just me. I scooted down the wall to unzip my backpack.

I was blind by the time I brought the bottle to my lips, but still somewhat alive. Slowly with shaking hands I drank the crimson liquid. The sweet taste of metal hit my tongue then filled my hollow veins.

THE DEMONIC EYES

Halfway through the gallon, the rose contracted giving me back my vision. Relief washed over me.

Tucking the jug back in the bag, I headed back to the street.

PEOPLE FADE BUT LOVE IS INFINITE

DAMIAN

My father was there that morning when I awakened. He had been grilling bacon, egg, and cheese sandwiches in a pan still dressed in pajamas.

"Hello, Damian," he said, seeing me.

"Hell—whoa," said my grumpy tired self. "What are you doin'?"

"Making breakfast before you go to school," he answered, which made me raise eyebrows. "You had quite the night terror last night. I thought you said you don't get those anymore."

"I don't," I lied.

"Well, you did."

I went to the bathroom and turned on the shower after glancing at myself in the mirror. My hair was a mess, sticking up in all kinds of odd directions. As I undressed, my fingers felt the skin of my cut arms. I seemed to get more each and every day. Some were now on my torso. It looked horrifying, but it was the only way to let the voices go.

Leaving the mirror, I went in the shower. The warm water stung the ones from last night, not yet crusted with dry blood. I couldn't believe I did this to myself. Sometimes it wasn't even from the voices, now I sometimes did it because I was bored. I knew no better than to hurt myself.

After my shower, I sat down at the table with fifteen minutes yet to spare. My dad served me, a cheeky smile upon his face. I did not return it.

"What's the matter?" he asked, sitting down.

"It's a Monday. What do you think?"

There was silence then he spoke, "You're not mad are you?" My eyebrow rose. "About my girlfriend?"

"I don't give a shit," I said. biting into my sandwich.

"Language," he warned.

"Not like you don't use it." I sipped my coffee. "What are you doing here, Dad?"

"What do you mean? It's my house."

"Then what am I doing here?"

"Damian…"

I cut him off before he could speak. "Dad, I don't want to live here anymore."

"Okay, then maybe we can move after…"

"No, dad. I don't want to live here with you."

His smile disappeared into a scorning frown. He wasn't okay with that. "What? You don't want to live here? Damian, you couldn't possibly know what you want. For heaven's sake, you're nothing but a child! What do you think you'll do, huh! Where are you going to go?"

"I don't care where I go." He began to yell over me, but I raised my voice louder. "Dad! Dad! Listen to me!" He got quiet for a moment, arms crossed across his chest. "You don't love me Dad."

"What do you mean I don't…"

"You don't love me, Dad! You don't. Where are you every night? Where have you been all this time? Huh, Dad. Where were you when Mom died!" This made him quiet. "Where were you when she decided to kill herself?" I was crying now, a frog stuck in my throat. "At work… because work is more important than your own family. It's more important than what she was going through. Did you even stop for a second to see what was wrong? No. You didn't. You say you changed, Dad. You haven't. Yeah, you've forgotten about her, but you've never recognized me."

One last look in his eyes and the sound of a honk was heard from outside. Before he could say anything, I grabbed my backpack, leaving him to think. I wiped the tears from my face, looking down so that no one could see my sullen eyes. I didn't even glance up at the bus driver who always had to make a comment.

"Move your slow ass a little quicker next time. I have stops to run, and you the last person I'd eva wait for."

I sat down in my usual seat. Billy breathed on the back of my neck. I didn't want to deal with him. I put my head to my knees, my hands covering my head, crying. A feeling of someone's skin against mine, I then felt that it was not a strike. It was gentle, reassuring.

Looking up, I saw it was Viper. I didn't even notice someone sitting next to me. Staring at me with those blue oceans of hers, she wiped away a tear from my cheek with a thumb. I had never seen her look at me like that before. I had never even had her touch me. Then I realized I had stopped crying, consumed by her beauty.

"You'll be okay," and that is all she said.

I felt okay until gym period. I was coming out of the shower, a towel wrapped around my waist. Going to my locker, I found it empty. Someone had taken my clothes. There I was standing there practically naked with three minutes to spare until class time.

"Hey," I asked, "has anyone seen my clothes?"

"No," said one guy and everyone else shrugged their shoulders.

I searched in the shower stall. You never know, maybe I had accidently brought them in there with me. Coming out with nothing, I began to search every nook and cranny. I came up with nothing, causing me to freak out. All I had was the sweatshirt that had been zipped up in fear of my cuts showing and the towel wrapped around my waist. Perhaps I could walk like this to the office and tell the principal that they did this, but it was embarrassing.

THE DEMONIC EYES

I hear the bell ring overhead, meaning I was late for next period. The PE teacher was nowhere to be seen, so I had to take the walk like a man. I grasped the towel tightly as I walked down the hall. Everyone's eyes were on me, laughs and giggles heard. My face turned red. I was mortified, but I had to get my clothes back.

Just then as I'm walking down the hall, there was a tug on my towel as a foot stomped down on it. I tripped. My towel fell to the ground, no longer on me. The laughter was louder this time as they saw me bare. There was pointing and name calling. At this point, I was far from mortified. I've dug a hole so far into embarrassment, there was no going back. My world was collapsing.

To make it worse, as I lay there on the ground, covering my bare ass, people began to surround me. Those people were Billy and his friends with a full set of sneer. I was going to die today. Not exactly how I wanted to die.

"Hey there, little freak," he said, nudging me with his foot. "Looking for these?" From behind him, he pulled out my shorts, dangling them in front of my face. I reached for them. He pulled them away before I could grasp them. "Sucker."

Billy tossed them away into the crowd, and I felt like I was going to cry. I should just give up now. *Get me away from these bastardly humans. Oh god, just let me die.* As the tears started to form, Billy began to kick me in the side of my torso and hip.

"Little girl, why don't you show us your gold mine. Huh, little girl." They kicked harder and harder. "You're nothing but a pussy. Come on, show us like you do with all the boys, you little faggot."

I covered my ears, my head to the tiled ground. As Billy kicked, the others took my arms to take of my sweatshirt. I tried to shake them off, but I don't fight enough. I don't want them to see my nakedness. Just then though, as my sweatshirt came off, I heard gasps. Then my remembrance of the scars hit me.

"Eww," some girl shrieked.

"What a fucking pathetic scum," declares Billy, "Ha ha. What a fucking freak."

I'm crying now onto the floor as he kicks harder into my rib cage. I can feel the bruise and I felt like my bones are going to crack any second. *Just let me die now surrounded by this torture. I can't take it any longer. Just look at the freak I am.*

I knew I was going to die. I knew it. Die lying there in my own tears. *Oh let me die. Just let me.*

Just then the lights went off. There was complete blackness. There was cussing and confusion, so much so that Billy stopped kicking. I got up from the ground. I couldn't see, but I could feel my way. Anywhere from here was better.

Soon I felt someone grabbed my arm, pulling me into another hallway. At first I was scared, thinking it was him, but I couldn't scream for a hand covered my mouth. Lips trembled near my ear, breath brushing against it.

"Shh," the female voice whispered, "don't scream."

The person pulled up my leg to stick it in my shorts then the other. She helped me to that, and I pulled it up the rest of the way. I don't need to ask to know who she was. What would this mean? Why would she help me?

She then touched my arms, making me put them up in the air. She put the shirt over me, and I shivered as her ice cold fingertips brush my side, the side I got kicked. She then brushed her thumb along my cuts as though she could wipe them away.

Had she been watching the whole time to know they were there? As there was nothing but silence in the dark, I didn't know what to say. She must have been disgusted too.

"Thank you," I whispered.

"This still doesn't make me your friend."

With that being her last words, she kissed me on the cheek. Yes, she kissed me for the second time. It just doesn't make sense. She hated me but she liked me. I wasn't sure these days whether she was a friend or an enemy, but all I could say regardless was that she helped me when no one else would.

The lights went back on, and she was gone. It was as if she hadn't been standing there.

I could hear the confused sound of Billy's voice. "Where'd he go?"

Before they could find out, I dashed down the hall, away from the crowd and out the front doors of the building.

I kept thinking about her that night, how she saved me. *Is she the one to turn off all the lights in the building?* Stupid questions like these ran through my head. Then there were the ones of why she was pushing me away. She was probably just a lonely person with no intention of being my friend. All she wanted was to tease me, and one day, her teasing will be like the way they treat me. But I couldn't think that. No, if that was true, then why would she strive to such lengths to help me. She could have started kicking me right then and there.

It finally shown true that I was falling in love with her, a girl I barely knew. Her eyes were hiding something. I saw it every once in a blue moon along with that smile. She was beautiful. I needed to know her. I wouldn't stop until I get to.

It was nine o'clock when I heard the sound of a truck pulling up. I didn't expect him to be home. I pulled out my earbuds as the car door slammed shut. An angry slam.

Recognizing that slam, I ran to the big closet in my room, locking both my door and closet. My heart pounded in my chest as I heard my father bursts through the entrance downstairs. I started shaking as the shouting started.

"Where are you, you little rat," exclaimed the drunk and angry man.

The sound of shattering bottles could be heard from downstairs.

"I'm gonna get you, and when I do, you better apologize to your father for being such an ungrateful bastard."

I covered my ears at his slurred words and heard a muffled sound and his boots slamming against the stairs. Tears that had welled up in my eyes brushed my cheeks. I thought this was over. I thought this was done. He was a changed man. He wanted to build his family again, get to know his son, have a wife that would be a good influence on me. No, I guess people never really change.

He hadn't touched a drop in over three years, but here he was, rolling back to it again. There he was now banging furiously at my bedroom door, with balled fist.

"Open the door, Damian," he yelled, "I'll show you the consequence of being an embarrassment. Open the door, you little faggot!"

He never got through that night. After an hour of swearing and hammering, he gave up everything, growing silent. I stayed in the closet in the far corner, behind the rack of clothing. I tried to sleep but I couldn't.

I ran my hands across the floor in search of something. Finally I found the tiny holes, and cracked open the door within the floor. I lifted it up to reveal a large cardboard box that had holes in it and a warm blanket I had since I was a child.

Wrapping the blanket around me, it still smelled fresh and clean. Comfortable. I ripped the tape off the opening of the box so I could peer inside. In it were a bunch of memories I kept. I flipped through all the pictures, all with smiles on their faces. First was of me, just a boy of five with a terrible haircut I had decided to give myself. Another was of my mother, a bunch of her actually. Then there was the one of someone I once called my friend.

His name was Carver. I had met him two years ago when he was a new student at my school. He had blue eyes and blond hair. He was a lot like me, but he was a lot friendlier. Being easier to talk to, we became friends easily.

After a few months though, something between us began to change. All my conscious thoughts began to revolve around him. I was beginning to fall in love with him. He felt the same.

I kept my relationship with him from my dad, from a lot of people. One night though it came out, and not the way I wanted it to. I had come home from school to find my father going through my pictures and the text messages on my phone. That's when the beatings happened. It started with an accidental punch in the face then it transgressed into a constant affliction.

Not shortly after, Carver became sick. First time it occurred, it happened at his house. He came out of the bathroom blood dripping down his face. When it happened again, his parents decided that they needed to move closer to the nearest hospital. It being far away, I never saw him again, never heard from him either. I'd like to think things are okay, that he's fine; but by the way his health was, I'm not too sure. It's something I'll never know.

Coming back to where I was, I heard a sound from within the box. Inside of the box was another box, but this one was made of oak wood. Hand carved, it had words encrypted on the top: *People fade but love is infinite.* With it was carved a bird. A few holes were on the sides of the box, and a sound of the creature traveling through them could be heard.

I popped the latch on the front of the box, pulling up the lid. Inside there was a mockingbird. Her right wing had been broken and it was wound together with a cast I had made her. As her eyes met mine I called her name, Isabel.

SUFFER

Viper

It was night, two days before Halloween, and I couldn't sleep or eat or do anything for that matter. Something had been troubling me, the Winters boy. There was a strange aura about him. He needed help and that was plain to see today.

"Stop pondering about him," said Tom as we sat at the dinner table. I barely touched my steak. "I told you not to get attached to a human. He is not our problem. Our problem is elsewhere."

"But father…"

"Do not father me," he ordered. "What is so important to you about him? Are you really going to blow our cover over a stupid boy? He already questions. They all are. And whose fault is that? They'll kill him too. Do you want that?"

"I want to kill him as much you did mom," I yelled. He looked shocked. "Or don't you remember she was human too? You knew the consequence. Didn't you?"

I pulled away from the table and ran up the stairs before he could spare another word. Locking my bedroom door, I let the music blare loudly but had no intention of listening to it. Escaping out the window, I ventured throughout the night.

I found him all alone on a park bench, shoulders slumped, looking over a box in his hand. Although his head was covered with his hood, I saw the tremble of his lips. As I sat down beside him, he didn't bother to look up. I could tell he knew it was me though.

"What do you want? You come to remind me why no one wants to be my friend? Just go away."

Wrapping my arm comfortingly around him, I moved my lips closer to his ear, "You have something you wish to confess. Well, I have something too. It eats at you like a disease you can't get rid of. Suffer alone or suffer together. It's your choice, but I don't want to suffer alone anymore."

After a gentle kiss met his cheek, he looked up at me. His eyes were so beautiful yet full of sorrow. Damian embraced me, slightly shaking from the coldness of the rain. We stayed like that for a while until I said we needed to get out of the rain and that he should probably go home.

"No," he said, catching my hand. "Please don't go. They don't like you because I do."

"They?"

"The voices," he said, eyes glancing downward in what seemed to be fear of judgment.

"I have the perfect place we can go," I said, assuring him everything was fine with a smile. He returned a slight smirk.

SCARS TOO DEEP TO HEAL

DAMIAN

I was at loss of words, so she did care. She had feelings for me, maybe not the way I wanted her to but at least she did.

By the time she brought me to the designated place, my hands had turned blue. She was just as pale as ever.

"You're not cold?"

"I'm never cold," she said. "We are here."

There we were at what seemed to be a playhouse made of wood and stone. It looked creepy; it being in the forest. At the same time though, it was a cute, a secret hideout to get away from the world.

Viper unlocked the padlock and opened the fragile-looking door. She escorted me inside and locked the door behind her. Everything was dark until she lit an old-fashioned lamp by the entryway.

It was small inside. Shelves on each far wall held miscellaneous items. On the wall before me were messages and drawings painted in only black and red.

"This is just the beginning," said Viper who then rolled the carpet from the floor. It revealed a trapdoor. From that door was a ladder leading downward. "Now this, this is what I'd like to call the best hideout ever."

After she went down, I moved down the ladder, cautious of my steps. She took the box from me and helped me down. Then she handed it back to me.

Turning, I saw what the whole fuss was about. The room was probably about the length of my house. Cement-blocked walls were built to support this underground study along with columns that held up the ceiling. Along the walls were bookshelves packed full. One was bare though, just like the ones upstairs, but this one had posters that could only be hers along with a giant map. In the middle of the room were red leather chairs and a table. To the left was a desk, papers scattered on it. In the far corner and to the right was a made bed.

"Wow," I said in awe. "This is amazing."

"Thank you. I repaired it. I usually sleep here when I want to get away. You are now welcome here."

We took a seat upon the bed and she asked me, "What's in the box?"

I stuttered for a moment, not sure if it was right to show her, "I-It's a…I mean it's nothing."

"Well, you would be quite strange, hauling around an empty box. If you don't want to show me, fine. It's okay," she said, her hand next to mine.

"It's the last thing my mother gave me before she died," I confessed. "She found it in the yard when she was in the garden. She said she couldn't let it die there so we could help it heal together." I lifted the lid for her to see the bird. "Her wings have been broken since. They don't seem to want to fix themselves." And I caught myself muttering, "Just like I don't."

I closed the lid of the box and felt something in my other hand. It was her hand interlocking with mine. Then she looked at me with those beautiful eyes. There was no smile on her face anymore.

"I saw your scars," she said.

"Oh, so that's why you want to be my friend all of a sudden… because you pity me," I assumed.

"No, I do not pity you," she said. "For I have some of my own."

She pulled up the sleeves of her sweatshirt, and I held back from gasping. These were real scars, stitched from years of torment. Cuts so deep, I don't know how she was able to hide them. I've seen her without long sleeves and never saw them before.

I ran my hands over them, feeling the indentations in her skin. I didn't know what to believe. She was a hard girl, rough around the edges, but I never expected her to be so downtrodden. Perhaps she had been through similar pain.

Next, I couldn't believe what she did. Viper lifted my head when I continued to stare down at my scars and brushed her fingers through my hair. I saw a short glimpse of her eyes until they closed. Mine closed too as she brought her lips to mine, pulling me closer. Our lips locked as I felt a slight tug on my hair. With her other hand, she slid up my shirt, feeling my abdomen.

I pushed away from her. "I'm sorry but this is too much."

Now I saw there were tears on her cheeks. I moved my hand to wipe them away, but she pulled back. I feared that I had upset her.

"It's not you, believe me. It's just I don't know you that well enough to kiss you like that."

"I wish you did," she replied with a sad glare.

"I don't understand," I said. "You pushed me away from being my friend, but now you want me more than that."

"I always wanted to know you, but it is forbidden."

"What do you mean forbidden?"

"My father is very selective. You wouldn't understand his reasons."

"Well, if I'm such a problem to him, I guess I'll leave."

"No," said Viper, catching my wrists as I was about to turn away. "Please stay. You're the only one who understands."

Seeing the loneliness in her eyes, I couldn't object. Besides, I felt like I needed her as much as she did me. Perhaps even more than she did. I couldn't go home now, and I didn't know when I'd build the strength to.

We fell asleep that night together, her arms wrapped around me. I'd never been this close to a girl before. All I could think about was that she had such a nice aroma and thinking of Carver. How it used to be like this. Then though, I was happy, scar free, and I wish I could be that again.

THE MARKINGS

Slayer

Another death, but this time, it were animals. From coyotes to pigs, the bodies were on the ground. A farmer was the first to discover his three little pigs dead. At first we thought it was the coyotes, but when we found one dead, it couldn't have been.

All the animals had similar characteristics: they had all been drained of their blood, slashed along the throat area. It was indeed a slash not a bite, leading to the conclusion that it couldn't have been the works of an animal.

"What do you think this is," asked the sheriff as we walked along the trail of dead pigs. "Do you think this is connected to our other case?"

"I know for a fact it is," I answered as I came to something carved into the dirt ground—a star within a circle and, next to that was a new symbol, an elaborate eye. "We know for a fact that the star represents Satanism, but the question is what does the eye mean?"

"I don't know," answered the sheriff. Then he turned toward the direction where a few FBI agents were. "Hey, we found something."

Sheriff was an idiot. He couldn't even conclude the simplest thing. I, on the other hand, knew exactly what the symbols meant. It was the whole reason I was here. Oh yeah, it was a cult all right. A cult I would finally get my hands on. There was no running now. I got them trapped.

YOU'LL CEASE TO EXIST

Damian

The next day, I woke at five and left a note for Viper before I snuck out. Hell yeah, I was terrified to go to school but I couldn't just miss the rest of the year. Besides, today was the day if anyone messed with me, I'd make sure they'd regret it. I was tired of people trying to push me around. *If they hit me I just got to hit them back. At least one hard punch.*

Adorned with an Avenged Sevenfold tee shirt, black skinny jeans, and Converse, I walked out of the house, backpack in hand. My father had been fast asleep on the couch. The whole living room smelled of piss, and I feared I'd had to clean that later.

On my way out, Wolfe rubbed her little body against my leg, knowing what had happened last night. "I know, girl, I got to go," I said and closed the door behind me.

I decided to walk to the school, trying to avoid the ridicule I would have gotten on the bus. It was good weather too, the sun was shining. I swear I hadn't seen the sun in ages. Maybe it was a sign that the day wouldn't be as bad as I thought. Hell, what was I thinking? They wouldn't forget and certainly mock.

I walked into English class a tad bit early, the only one in the room except for Mr. Franklin. "Damian, can I talk to you for a second?"

Ugg. I knew that was coming. I placed my books on my desk and then went up to him. "Yes, Mr. Franklin?" I clearly didn't want to talk about yesterday, so I hoped he wouldn't mention it. In fact, he didn't at all. "I read your essay this morning, and if there is anything I can do for you, just ask. I know it's hard growing up without a mother. I lost mine when I was three, and my father wasn't exactly the kindest, most attentive man. If you have any other problems, presumably like yesterday or anything outside school grounds, it's okay if you tell me about it." There was a long, dragged-out pause with him just staring at me as if he knew I had something to confess, but when I didn't, he said, "That is all."

I turned to take my seat, but he added one more thing, "And don't mention anything to anyone."

"Not a peep."

In that class, we were assigned to write a poem. I was pretty amazing when it came to poetry, but I couldn't write a story longer than ten pages for my life. We were given thirty-five minutes, and in those minutes, all I could focus on was the fact Billy and his accomplices weren't in school. *Had they been suspended or even expelled?*

The timer rang, telling us time was up. A few people read. One girl had written a poem about shoe shopping. Honestly, it was the stupidest poem I had ever heard. There was nothing truly poetic in shoe shopping, but if it made her herself, then that's it. Then some guy got up and recited his poem about football. Now this was a little more tolerable, for it was pretty well written as far as football went, and he seemed to have passion for it. Then some geeky kid came up with this poem about psychics. I was so lost within it I had no idea what he was talking about. Then Mr. Franklin called up Viper. This had my full attention. She recited:

"I walk throughout the starry night,
Wondering where did the time go.
Every day part of us leaves,
Within our dream infested sleep.
I sit there wondering in the dark,
What becomes of us?
Not just in life but within death,
Where does our journey take us?
It's true that people change,
Just like the seasons do.
And I watch as those so kind
Become nothing but cruel.
Whether your thoughts are cruel,
Or ever so kind,
If you wonder too long
In your thoughts or dream infested sleep,
You'll cease to exist like the person you used to be."

There was silence from the classroom, as if perhaps they couldn't comprehend or were stunned by the fact she had talent to write. Then there was applause from Mr. Franklin, who said, "That was great."

As she took a seat next to me, all I could think about was, *What did she mean?* Perhaps we change in fear that every day we are closer to dying. Every day we wonder what is to become of ourselves after. And whatever you are, kind or cruel, if you think too much about what lies beyond, you begin to lose yourself.

I felt her poem was something I can relate to, wishing every day that I'd died. Still I don't because I fear what is to become of me. If I think too much about all the wrongs and of death's door, I felt I couldn't be saved, but maybe perhaps I hadn't wondered that far yet.

When I had gotten home and after cleaning the mess my father made in the living room, I got a phone call.

"Hey, it's Miles," he said in a tune I didn't expect. I assumed he would be like "*Tell me what's wrong!*" but it was just the opposite. "How you doing, kid?"

Horrible. My father's an abusive drunk, screwing around with unknown woman. I have cuts all over my body that were exposed to everyone in school yesterday. I basically wake up terrified to seize the day, but yeah, I got a band and a girl likes me. How are you?

"All right, I guess," I replied.

"That's great," he said. "So tomorrow's Halloween. I was wondering if you wanted to come to this party I'm having. I mean there's alcohol, but nobody has to know about that. What you think?"

"Uh sorry, Miles," I said, letting him down, "but I kind of have another party I'm going to."

"Where?"

"The Johansson household."

"Are you serious? That house. Why? Are you friends with them or something?"

"Viper invited me," I said, and there was a slight chuckle on the other end.

"The boy finally got a girlfriend. That's great. I'll see you Saturday… if I don't have a hangover."

HALLOWEEN

Damian

It was the night of the Halloween party, and I had been standing there staring at my full-length mirror. I hadn't participated in this since I was like ten. You reach a certain age, and then people start throwing you off the porch, so the only time to celebrate Halloween was really a party.

This evening I was a vampire. Now I wasn't one of those stereotypical vampires or the ones that sparkled in the movies. I mean I was what I would imagine a vampire to look like. Now they would blend in with the crowd by day; but by night, when they are thirsty, they would be quite creepy and dark (like me).

I was quite proud of myself. I should say especially with the makeup. It looked so realistic. The blood streamed down my face in lines from my lips. It stained my white shirt a bit. With that I wore black jeans that had chains dangling on the sides. My hair was spiked upward in the back to make it all mysterious. Around my eyes I put a blue color to make my skin appear even paler and dead. I made cut lines with the makeup to make it look like I got bit there. It was so close to my other scars that I decided for once to wear a short-sleeved shirt in public. They were healed to the point there were only a few of them left, faint as claw marks.

I had been changing quite a lot in the last few weeks. I noticed my ability to heal is abnormal. My cuts were pretty deep. In a matter of four days, they are nothing but scratches. The ones on my legs are still there, but that's because they are fresh. Not just that, I was having trouble keeping food down. In fact, I haven't really eaten anything in a week, but I didn't get any skinnier. I am still so fat.

I looked at my watch. It's time to go. Like usual, my father waltzed in the door, no guilt whatsoever evident on his face, as I was coming down the stairs. With a cheeky smile he asked, "What the hell are you wearing?"

"I'm going out."

He still stood by the door, keeping his ground. He looked less happy now. I guess he forgot about yesterday. He always did. "Where are you going?"

"Out. Now move."

I practically pushed him aside and ran out the door before he could catch me. Behind me he closed the front door giving in.

She scared the shit out of me when she came out of the woods and onto the path. Viper had fake blood dripping down her face. It was dark, and I could barely see, but it smelled odd. I could smell it as I was standing next to her. She wore a white dress splattered with blood, and there was blue around her eyes too.

"You scared me," I said with a staggered breath.

She looked at me wide eyed, as if I wasn't supposed to see her there coming out of the woods. When the look faded, she said, "Oh hey… I wanna to show you something."

"Okay."

She took my hand after wiping it on her dress and led me down the path. We came to a gate just as big as the one at the beginning of the trail. She broke the chain from it and led me inside.

The place she wanted to show me was a garden far behind the back of the house. It was unlike anything I have seen for it was October, and the flowers looked as though they had just bloomed yesterday. The roses were a bright shade of crimson, the violets a deep purple. There were high bushes surrounding the flowers from outside. It looked as if perhaps this was a maze.

"It's a maze garden," Viper said. "It was here when we moved, but I was the only one to find it."

"How can no one know about it? It's in the back of your house."

"Yeah well, it's a little far. If you don't go down the hill, you'll never see it. And I like to think there is a bit of dark magic to it."

"Dark magic." Now I was starting to think she was a little crazy but then I remembered the computer at the library. This is still part of that house. "What do you mean?"

"Well, when I came across it, I thought it was so beautiful that I went to get my brother to show it to him. But when we got on the hill, we looked down, and Drake didn't see it. All he saw was the pond on the other side. So I guess the garden's my little secret. Our little secret now."

I didn't know whether to believe it or not. It sounded insane. Perhaps there was more than the disappearance and fires in this place.

"What's in the middle?"

"Come on. I'll show you," she said.

After about ten minutes, she led me to the center of the garden. In it, all surrounded by flowers, was a gazebo. Viper took my hand and brought me to the gazebo.

"It's a nice place to be especially when you want to get away from all the havoc."

She moved over to one of the benches where a record player lay. Viper moved the handle, turning it on. Slow classical music played in the air.

"Care to dance?" she asked, holding out her hand.

"I'd love to."

I rested my hands on her waist, hers on my shoulders. Then we swayed back and forth. I've never slow danced with anyone before. I was surprised I wasn't tripping over her feet.

She was so close to me that I could smell the aroma again. At first there was a whiff of something rotten wavering in my nostrils, but then there was a sweet pleasant smell. I wasn't sure if it was her or of the roses around us. I had to break the silence.

"You're freezing. Do you need a sweater?" and just when I asked that, I looked down at her arms to see the marks she had shown me were gone.

"I never get cold."

"Viper?"

"Yes?"

"What happened to your scars? They are gone."

"I've covered them that is all."

"Oh," I commented, feeling stupid. What did I think that they just got up and walked away?

There was a silence between us. She was staring back into my eyes. The creepy ballet music played as we swayed back and forth.

"You probably think I'm strange," she said, "but I feel a strong emotion toward you. I'm not sure what it is but I find myself thinking of you many times."

"I find myself doing the same thing. You are very beautiful. You shouldn't like someone like me. I'm such a disgrace."

I look away from her toward the ground, but she put a hand to my cheek, directing me to look at her.

"I do not believe in love at first sight. I don't really believe that love exists. It's just chemistry of the brain. People leave one another all the time over the smallest issues. If one really loved another truly, they would stay inseparable. But perhaps we were chosen to cross paths for a reason. I don't know exactly what reason yet, but it must be of importance."

There was pause and then I spoke something I meant to say earlier, "You write beautifully."

"Thank you."

"I've been thinking about it and wanted to know. What do you think is out there? Do you believe in heaven?"

"Yes. But it won't have me and neither will hell," she answered. "You wouldn't understand Damian. I'm not a nice person. Not like you think I am."

"And how so?"

"I can't tell you. All you got to know is that I'm on your side. Okay?"

"Okay," I answered quizzically.

"Have you ever fallen in love, Damian, truly?"

"Once," I answered, "but we were separated."

"Death?" she asked, and I could almost feel her breath on my lips.

"I don't know. Disease took him away," I said too fast before I realized what I said. Now she would judge me forever. How could I have been so stupid?

"My heart too was torn. My friend, she was killed in a car accident. I really felt for her that emotion but…she never got to know. I don't fall in love anymore because, every time I do, someone gets hurt, and I don't want that."

I was shocked that she too was the same as me. "That's terrible, and I don't seem to understand. If you do not love, then why are you always there when I'm not expecting it, when I am sad, always trying to help me and wanting to kiss me so terribly? What am I to you, huh? First you say that you can't stand to be near me, and the next your all over me."

"I told you, my father doesn't like people like you, but I've always felt something. I knew you'd be the only one who'd understand me and accept me for who I am. I just can't tell you everything about me yet. Is that understood?"

I realize now that we had stopped dancing and the record was skipping. After a deep sigh, Viper said, "I haven't had friends in a long time, so would you like to go to a party, best friend?"

"I want to be more than friends," I muttered but she heard me.

"I thought you did too, but you're so impossible."

Getting louder now, I said, "Why don't you just tell me what is truly on your mind 'cause frankly, you are such an emotional confused wreck that I have no idea what I even am to you. You are such a tease; it angers me."

"I fancy you," she finally said with a devious smile. "Is that close enough to what you're looking for?"

I nodded because now I understood. "I fancy you too."

THE DEMONIC EYES

She escorted me to the house; we walked hand in hand. There were so many people there. I was surprised she had those many friends.

"Brother's friends," she explained, "and their friends and so on."

Now that I can see Viper better compared to the darkness of our meeting place, I saw she was wearing a short sleeveless white dress. It had ruffles and was tattered, stained with fake blood, quite realistic blood. She wore no leggings. On her feet were combat boots. I tried not to stare, but she had really gorgeous legs.

"Hey," said someone approaching us, which made me look up. She was a blond Victoria Secret angel (It was her costume). She wasn't half as beautiful as Viper. She had a cup in her hand filled with a golden liquid, the other a slice of pizza. "Viper, I didn't know you had a boyfriend? That's so cute. Aw, don't they make just an adorable couple? Little girl's got a date."

"You talk to me," she said, "like I'm younger than you ever again, I'll shove that pizza so far up your ass, you'll be speaking Italian." With a finger, she made a sweeping motion across her throat.

"Ooh," said her brother, coming up behind her, "that's a good one, sis. Real mature. Who's this trash?"

"None of your fucking business, and what is that in your hand," she said, pointing to the bottle he was grasping.

"It's called a beer, girlfriend. You should know plenty about that."

"You know you're not supposed to be drinking," she stated, arms crossed.

"Yeah, but you can?"

"I'm older than you and hell a lot more responsible. You know what father said. You can't control your anger when you're drunk."

"Come on, sis, it's a party. Have a little fun for once. Besides I'm only a year younger than you."

"Fine," she agreed. "But if anyone touches the Jack, I'll kill them."

She storms away with me and I have plenty of things running through my head. So apparently Viper was a drinker. Her brother was a bit of a dickhead and that she was older than him. Also she was into hard liquor. That was shocking to me. She didn't seem the type.

Loud music was blaring crappy pop tunes. There were bright flashing disco lights and a disc jockey stood on the balcony. I noticed the architecture now. Two staircases came up on both sides to form a U shape. Some people were upon the balcony, which Viper didn't seem to be happy with. It was hard to tell what the house looked like with all the people in it.

As we got up the stairs, I heard the sound of something breaking, probably a vase. This made Viper quite annoyed. "Father is going to hear this."

We go off to the left hall leading me to another hallway. In it there was nothing but doors. A long red carpet fanned out on the floor. Little lights hung beside each doorway. There was nothing creepy about this house. It was elegant. Some people hung in the hallway in line for the bathroom, ready to puke their insides.

Viper opened her bedroom door to see two people in it, a guy and a girl making out on her bed. They looked up when they heard the door. "Get the fuck out!"

"What figures, man?" asked the guy.

"Get out!"

They scampered out the door, and she shut it behind them. "There was not supposed to be this many people here. He's going to kill me." She paused. "Whatever! Let's have fun, but I'm not going out there. Too many bodies."

"You want a drink?" she asked. "Anything from water to whiskey."

"Anything is fine."

After she came back with a bottle a Jack and two red solo cups, I was hesitant. "I never had one of these before."

"Great, I want to see your face."

I sighed then took it in my hands. I tipped it back and felt an extreme burn down my throat. I coughed in reaction, making Viper laugh.

"It tastes weird the first time," she said.

I set the cup down still trying to debate whether it was nasty or not. "So is it the party life you don't want to talk about?" I asked.

"Not exactly," she answered and changed the subject. "Would you like to dance?"

"I would love to. I mean…like to."

She smiled and took my hand. Just as she did, a slow song came on. This time as we danced, she wrapped her arms around my neck as we swayed back and forth.

She stared into my eyes, and all I wanted to do was kiss her. Then when the end of the song came, she leaned in closer. She stayed there lingering for I had asked her to stop trying to kiss me before. Now I wanted her to. I wanted all of her. Perhaps it was too early to want, but I knew enough to know that I was in love with her. Sure, she had secrets, but so did I.

I took her by the chin and pressed her soft lips against mine. I kissed her passionately like never before. Then she kissed me back, pulling me tighter. I didn't want it to end, but then there was a scream.

Viper was the first to pull away. She stood there for a moment as if determining what kind of scream sounded. It wasn't any scream of some obnoxious drunk. It was a woman's scream of bloody murder.

Through the door she dashed out of the room, and I followed. We pushed past people to find out what all the commotion was about. When we got to the scene, I couldn't believe my eyes. Outside on the lawn, a young man and woman were hanged on a tree. Each of their eyes had Xs slashed in them.

Viper remained silent staring at the people with shock in her eyes. Those inside tried to peer through the windows. The girl that had discovered them ran to her boyfriend burying her face on his chest.

A moment later, Viper yelled in an angry tone, "Drake! Drake!"

He came outside, oblivious, buckling the belt of his pants. "What?" Then he looked at where Viper was pointing. "Oh my god."

"Get them out. Call father and the police. Now!"

The police soon came to the scene. They didn't look the least bit horrified. One of them even said, "Oh great, not again."

"Not again?" I asked. "This happened before?"

He never replied, and just then another vehicle pulled up. A seal of the FBI was painted among the door. This was real serious. So this had been happening and no one had addressed it to the public. Was that even legal?

"We need all of you to come down to the station," said the sheriff of police, and giant nerves hit me. What would my dad do when he saw me being driven in a police car? Where was he now? "We just need to investigate you."

"So explain what happened. You had a party," said the sheriff and an FBI agent sitting across from us at the table. "Where were your parents?"

"My father was visiting an old friend of his," answered Viper.

"Your mother?"

"She died a long time ago."

"I'm sorry to hear that," he said, the female agent was jotting down notes. "So where were you when this was going on?"

"I was dancing," said Hunter.

"Oh, you weren't just dancing. You had alcohol. I could report that, but as long as you remain truthful, I'll let it slide. There were too many people there drinking, and I'm not on any mission to hunt them all down. Is that right?"

"Yes, sir. I had a few drinks."

The sheriff looked to Viper. "I was with Damian. We were just in my room dancing."

"Dancing in your room? That's all?"

"Yes. Can't a guy and girl just dance in ones bedroom without there being speculation of something else taking place?"

"That's not what I was inferring but well enough. Did any of you see or hear anything suspicious before the incident?" We all shook our heads and the sheriff sighed. "Well, I guess that's it for now. You may go."

Outside in the lobby, I met Tom's acquaintance. He didn't seem too thrilled. I mean why would anyone?

"What were you thinking, huh," yelled Tom, "having all those people at the house?" He then looked beyond them and saw me. Somewhat changing his tone but not like the night I had met him, he said, "Oh, hello, Damian."

I smirked, but he did not return a smile. It became the clear truth that he didn't like me. Why though? What was so wrong about me? *Everything. You're nothing but a loser. She doesn't even love you. You heard her. She hates you.*

As I awkwardly stood there, the voices were beginning to devour me. I was staring at the floor when I heard his voice.

"Huh?"

"Come on. I'll drive you home."

After the awkwardly quiet drive home, I went to my bedroom. Dad wasn't home as usual, probably with his girlfriend. I couldn't believe that he could get one, and I couldn't. What was she even to me?

I wasn't sure what was stranger Viper or the goddamn house. What was with the whole garden? The murder? Everyday life made less sense. It sucked. I couldn't get even one girl to truly love me. My father hated me, and I hate him. I'm afraid to go to school. In this world, it's not okay to be myself. Maybe, just maybe, everyone's life would be better if I just left.

I tried to turn out the thoughts I was having by turning the television on, but a soap opera came on that didn't make me feel any better. There was a father and a son arguing.

Father: Why can't you just be normal? Huh? Why do you have to be this freak? I don't get it. Drew, you've liked girls since kindergarten. What is this now, in spite?

Son: No, Dad. You don't understand. This is who I am.

Father: No, it is not. Any boy that sucks face with another boy is not mine! (He threw a picture of the two boys on the boy's lap of them,) See what all those years of living with your mother has done to you.

I flipped the channel. The show was too much like my actual life. It was horrifying. The next program that came on was of an old lady in a rocking chair reading what looked like a children's storybook. I was about to change it again, but then I heard something I didn't expect.

"They are watching you, boy. He is watching. The other will come for you."

What kind of freaking, wacked—"Beware, Damian." Now the woman was looking up at me with blood dripping from her eyes. "They're coming Damian! They're coming!"

The woman then seemed to be choking on something. There she died in the rocking chair on my TV screen.

INVOLVED

Damian

I awoke with a jolt. My curtain was flapping around violently in the air as water streamed into my room. As I got up to close it, thunder sounded and lightning cracked.

I sat there on the edge of my bed, trying to comprehend if Halloween really happened. The old woman couldn't have been real but was everything else?

As I wondered in complete confusion, I glanced down at my arms to see fresh slices. So that was that, the TV scene hadn't been real. Then what happened when I came home? Why did I do this? I told myself I would stop so I wouldn't become what she wanted me to avoid. But I couldn't. I can't. The pain was like a drug. I feel like I need it. Like if I don't do it, the voices only get louder.

Sitting there, I felt something in the pit of my stomach, an aching sensation. Soon it rose within me and I dashed to the bathroom. Sick to my stomach, I belched red liquid. I hadn't drunk anything red. Then I feel it on my tongue, the taste of the salt. I was sick just like

Carver was. No, I couldn't be, but a healthy person doesn't just throw up blood.

I turn on the light above the sink to wash my hands and face. There I saw in the crease of my elbow something I had never seen before. I hadn't even noticed it when I saw the cuts. There was this stringy black thing inside the crease of my elbow. It resembled how roots look like in the ground, tangled together yet growing in separate directions. Yes, it was growing but only for a second until it came to a halt, staying one size.

Putting to words what it was, was impossible. At that point, I had no idea what was wrong with me, physically and mentally. Once I looked in the mirror and smiled, a happy-go-lucky kid. Now all I saw was a frowning figure covered in scars and now this. When did I go wrong?

The next day, I woke up hoping it was a dream, but the black virus thing was still inside me. I zipped up my sweatshirt, and Wolfe looked at me with a concerned glare. Ignoring it, I gave her breakfast then bid her good-bye as the horn of Mile's car beeped.

"These are some badass songs, man," said Vic, reading them over. "All we need to do is write instrumental music to go along with it then we can get some gigs."

"Boss," said Ace, giving me a high five.

"So Miles told me that you have a girlfriend?" he said, changing the subject.

"Um yeah. I guess," I said.

"Just wondering. Does she have any single friends?"

Roxxi rolled her eyes behind his back.

"No," I answered, not mentioning she doesn't have any friends.

"I heard what is going on in your hometown. That must be quite scary, living with a serial killer and not even knowing it. Who do you think it is?" asked Vic which made everyone's ears perked up.

"I don't know, honestly," I said. "But I hope they find him soon."

THE DEMONIC EYES

So by the end of the day, we wrote the instrumental parts to two songs then Miles was driving me back home.

"Hey, I want to show you my place," he said, "if you have the time."

I had assumed that Miles lived at his college dorm, but apparently he did not. He had moved out of his parent's house a while ago. I hadn't known that. After hearing that, I expected an apartment; but no, he had a house, a nice house.

The lawn had been freshly cut. Bushes lined the house on either side of the porch. The house was pretty much surrounded by woods. As you drove by you saw tree, tree, tree, house then more trees. A red convertible was in the driveway. Working at a coffee shop, I was surprised he could afford all of this.

We walked into the house, and Miles offered to take my jacket and hang it up in the closet.

"Uh, no thanks," I said nervously.

"It's okay," said Miles. "No one is going to judge you here."

I gave him my jacket, my heart thumping wildly in my chest. He simply hung it, not a glance at my cuts, but then his lips moved, which scared me. In the end, he didn't say anything about the scars. "What's with the bruise?"

He had meant the black spot. It had been so early in the morning when I discovered it. I must have forgotten about it.

"Oh, I must have fallen."

Buying it, he led me deeper into his establishment. To the left of me was a kitchen. To the right was a reading area, chairs in the middle of the room, and shelves lined the wall.

Miles waltzed into the kitchen and opened the fridge. He pulled out a pitcher of iced tea.

"You like iced tea?" he asked.

"Yes."

After he poured me a glass, we went to the living room/band room. It was a lot darker in there but still very cleanly. Miles placed his iced tea on the counter and pulled something out of the back of the room. Unzipping a case, he revealed a guitar.

"Do you know what this is?" he asked.

"An electric guitar."

"Yes, an electric guitar signed only by Jimi Hendrix."

"Wow," I said and was about to ask him where he had got it when the door across the room opened.

Out walked a man. He was about Miles age with brown hair that swooped to one side. He had dark eyes, a few piercings, and tattoos. He was a lanky fellow. A towel wrapped around his waist for he had just gotten out of the shower.

"Um who's this?" asked the guy, meaning me.

"Oh, Jace. This is Damian, Damian Winters. You remember hearing about him, right?"

This whole situation was uncomfortable. One, I had no idea of this Jace. Second, most of all, he was hot as hell and not wearing any clothes, which made me feel kind of weird. Lastly, his eyes were searching me, staring all over, probably at my scars. The feeling of judgment was one of my biggest fears and I was seeing right now he was judging me as hard as he could.

"I do recall hearing about him," said Jace. Now I noticed he is British. "I didn't picture him to look like this though." Oh, there were the words. *What's with your skin, kid?* But then I heard him mutter, "Adorable."

I thought I was hearing things wrong, but no, that was what he said. Then for all of us to hear, "I'm going to put some clothing on."

He then left and Miles looked to me. "I'm sorry. I thought he wouldn't be home."

"Whatever," I said, which came out kind of angrily.

"He doesn't care, Damian. It's cool."

"Who is this Jace?"

"He's my roommate and friend. I met him at a concert."

Soon Jace came back into the living room, and my heart thumped wildly. *He's staring at me.* He wasn't though. He had been staring at the newspaper in his hands. His lips were parted, moving as though reading, but no sound came out.

"Mate, you do know you're in the paper," he finally said, glancing at me.

"What?"

He handed it to me. My eyes first caught the heading: "Murder Found at the Old Newman's House." My name was mentioned in it as quote "involved with incident" along with Viper and Drake. *Involved. What was "involved" supposed to mean? We didn't kill these people.*

Miles took the paper from my hands, reading it over. After he did, he looked to me. "The way they worded this, I don't know. It's as if they believe you did this."

"I...we didn't have anything to do with it. We heard a scream and went outside, and that's what we saw." I was shaking now. *We told them everything we knew. Did they really think we murdered them?* "It must have been a typo. Maybe they have their facts messed up."

"Hey," said Miles calmly. He dropped the paper. It fluttered to the ground. Putting a hand to my shoulder, he looked directly into my eyes. "Kid, I am with you every step of the way. I know that you didn't do this. If they accuse you, arrest you, I'll be there fighting by your side. I know there are things that you are not telling me, but I know it can't be this."

"I never saw those people in my life. They are a lot older than me, so even if they went to my school, I wouldn't be anywhere near them. It's too big of a place."

I was sweating now.

"I know, Damian," he said. "Now can you tell me what you are hiding?"

"No, I'm sorry. I can't." My eyes glanced away. "You would judge me if you knew, and you'll say things to people and then they'll come after me because you did. They'll take me away."

"Where would they take you?" he asked, a confused look on his face.

My heart was pounding in my chest now, sweat dripping down my skin. "I have to go."

"Tell me, Damian," he said, gritting his teeth. I got up from the couch to run away, but he caught my arm in a tight grip. "Damian, I swear if you killed them..."

"I didn't," I yelled. "The only person that deserves to be killed is me."

I can't believe the words came out of me, but they were too late to take back. He let go of my arm, and I ran to the closet. I grabbed my jacket. Throwing it on, I ran away from the house. Tears streamed down my cheeks. The sky then turned grey, raining on the earth.

NEWSPAPER BOY

Slayer

Writing the article went well. As soon as all of them were printed, I tied the bandana around my face, put on shades, and made sure a hood covered my face. It was 3:00 a.m., but I may never know when someone might see my face. Riding on a bike, I threw the new edition of the paper at people's doorsteps. By the final one, I rubbed my hands together, a smug smile upon my face. *Fall into my trap, boy. That's it. Just some time and everyone will know.*

I would finally get the others too, the ones I had been looking for, for years. All I had to do was talk with sheriff. He would fall for anything. They couldn't hide from me now. *Slayer's coming.*

LIPS SEWN SHUT

Damian

I didn't know what to do. I mean, the police were possibly looking for me, for us. I had to find her.

I ran down the trail to her house and knocked on the giant doors. There was no answer. Next was the garden. No one there either, which left one place.

Running through the woods, it was getting dark. The sun had almost set on the horizon. I tripped over my own feet, landing on the ground. A tingling sensation filled my arms. Leaves were now in my hair.

I was about to get up when I heard it, the sound of a twig snapping behind me. At first I presumed it was an animal, but as I saw its shadow hovering over me on the ground, I gulped a mouthful of saliva.

Turning my head, I saw a figure in a black cloak. Yes, a full cloak. As my eyes first lay upon it, I could have sworn I saw the eyes glow red. Heat rose within me. *What does this thing want? Is he going to kill me?*

When it took off its hood, I saw it was a man. A pretty normal-looking guy. He was tall, over six feet. He had brown hair and his face was quite scruffy. The only thing odd was that his hazel eyes looked almost gold.

"Hey, son, you all right?" he asked with a bit of a lisp.

The man held out his hand. I hesitated to grasp it. When I did, the man picked me up off my feet. I wipe off the dirt and crumbles of leaves from my arms. When I looked back up, the man was gone as if he had never stood there.

I glanced all around, but all I saw were trees. My mouth was agape. Then I crinkled my eyebrows, my palms up as if to say "where did he go." Dropping the subject, I traveled onward to find the secret hideout.

She was sitting down reading a book when I climbed down the ladder. Startled, she threw the book to the floor. She then kicked it under the chair as if she didn't want me to see what she was reading.

"What are you doing here?" she asked, a little panicky.

"You said I was welcome here," I answered. I had never seen her out of a state of calmness. "Did you read the paper today?"

"Why would I read the paper?"

"They suspect us," I revealed. "It said that we were involved."

"Maybe they mean that we were a witness." Her eyes looked grave.

"No." I let out a deep breath. "They suspect us of the murder. What are we going to do?" I start losing myself, pulling at my hair. I held back the tears in the corners of my eyes as I started to talk mostly to myself. "I couldn't kill anyone, and why, why did I say that to him. He's gonna send me somewhere. He's gonna want people to help me, but I don't need it. They don't care. Nobody cares..."

Viper wrapped her arms around me. I wrapped mine around her waist. "Everything is going to be okay," she assured in her soft, soothing voice. "All we got to do is keep *cool*." The word seemed alien, coming from her lips. "Can you do that?"

I nodded.

"Damian?"

Say you love me. Say you love me.

"I care about you, and I swear if you die, I'll die too."

She kissed my cheek, and my nerves feel all out of place. It wasn't exactly what I wanted to hear, but it was more than I expected.

"We're going to be okay."

"Viper," I asked, "what were you doing in the woods Halloween night?"

"Just walking. That's all. Why?"

"Were you here?"

"No," she said, getting out of our embrace. I never wanted her to.

"You go to the woods a lot."

"You watch me," she half exclaimed.

I scratched the back of my neck, blushing. "Yeah, I…I ah…sometimes. You didn't want to be my friend but I…"

"I understand," she said. "Can you promise me something, Damian?"

"What?"

"Don't ever come to or leave this place at night. When the sun sets, don't even think of setting foot into the forest."

"It is night now," I pointed out.

"So you must stay."

The next day, after I had awoken intertwined in Viper's arms, we headed to her house, running. I don't know if it was in fear of what took place in these woods or because we needed to find them before they were caught.

Slowing down at the house, Viper said to me, "Stay behind me. The house might not like you."

What was that supposed to mean? I remember back to the incident in the library and wondered what if there was something in that house I didn't know about? "We are watching you." *Who is this "we"?* I indeed needed to find out. First, the things I had read about the past here, the whole occurrence, and the fact that Viper seemed somewhat scared of this place made me wonder what was this big secret everyone was hiding. Even the neighbor across the street looked grave, staring at the house. It hit me, *the neighbor. She would know everything about here. Focus, Damian. Focus on yourself now. You have enough on your hands.*

Viper pried open the heavy door then we entered. Now that there are no partying bodies in the room, I saw the house completely. It was elegant just the same. It didn't seem like a mad house. It was far too quiet.

A sparkling chandelier hung from the ceiling. Before us were two stairs that came together in a U shape, leading to the second floor. Lining the walls were paintings, but no pictures of the family. Everything looked kind of bare.

Viper looked off into the distance as she was listening for something. Then I heard the sounds of footsteps echoing so loud, it was as if there was a person walking toward us, but there was no one else in the room but ourselves.

Without a word, she took my hand. A tingling sensation stung my fingertips, my whole arm, and then the center of my chest. Guiding me up the stairs, she led me to a door. With the twist of a knob, she revealed a chamber of books.

A man with brown hair, chest covered in tattoos, sat among a black couch. As we entered, he looked up, book in hand. The setting looked a little odd for such a man reading a cooking book.

"Father, where is brother?" Viper asked.

"Hey," said a voice behind her. A redheaded boy appeared.

"We need to discuss." She closed the door behind him, and we all sat down, Tom and Drake on one side, us on the other. "As you know, there has been murders taking place here. Of course we were interrogated, but apparently, we are not done with this case. We personally are suspects."

"If we are suspects then why didn't they take us just then," asked Drake, raising his eyebrows in disbelief. He was slouched over, his hand on his chin. "Why give us the chance to run?"

"I believe they didn't want us to know about this. They want to analyze us from afar, but some newspaper writer blurted out things they shouldn't have. Perhaps they even twisted the information they were told around. It wouldn't be like the police to give them information like that."

"Trust me this town's a bunch of idiots," I said. "They would."

"Not if they want to be on the FBI's good side."

With this, I nodded in agreement. "Valid point."

"What do we do? We need to run, get out of here," said Drake nervously.

"No," objected Tom. "I'm the father here. I say what goes. Everyone just keep calm and act like nice average people…not like you know you're being watched. Eventually, they'll realize we didn't do this, and they'll leave us be."

A switch went on in my head. It was kind of like what Viper said but the way he worded it was strange. *"Nice average people…not like you know you're being watched." Suspicious folks.*

After a moment of silence, Tom said, "Is that all?"

"Yes, father," she said, walking out of the room while holding my hand.

As I exited the room, I felt the eyes upon me, his eyes burning holes in the back of me. *Don't take it personally. I hate your kind, but don't take it personally.*

"I guess this is our parting," said Viper as we got to my doorstep.

"Why not stay for dinner," I insisted.

Opening the door, I was relieved that the house is clean. Wolfe walked passed me toward Viper as though I didn't even exist. Reaching her hand out, she patted her head.

"You didn't tell me you had a cat." She smiled.

Wolfe purred loudly. "Yeah. Sometimes I feel that she's my only friend."

"Well," Viper said, taking her hand away from Wolfe, "now you have two." There was a moment of silence as we walked to the kitchen. I was fiddling with the fridge and looking at her. She gave a half smirk which turned into a real smile. I never saw such a beautiful smile.

Everything was great right there in that moment. We danced, music blaring. We listened to a few of the songs my band wrote. She loved them, and I saw that smile again. It was so reassuring, that smile. Everything is going to be all right because I have her. Maybe I didn't have her exactly the way I wanted her, but she kept coming back, which I guess counted for something.

I thought this was going well but then it wasn't.

THE DEMONIC EYES

She was talking to me as I was cutting up the steak. I must have gotten distracted because the knife slipped from my hand. I hadn't noticed at first but then there was the burning, stinging sensation.

This pain wasn't a good pain. It didn't help me, just hurt a lot.

I looked down at the cut. It was deep, an oozing giant line across my hand. The blood poured out of it, dripping on the floor. For a second I stood there staring at it, shocked.

I looked to Viper. Her eyes were grave, staring down at the dripping blood. Her hands were cringing, fingers moving as one has in a seizure.

"Viper," I asked, slightly scared. "Viper?"

Her arms were shaking, fingers flexing. I could have sworn I saw a stream of red in the corner of her eye. I had never seen anything like it. I wasn't sure what to do.

Then she said in a low voice. "Stay away from me."

With a blink, she ran out the door.

MY FINAL SUICIDE NOTE

Damian

That night I lay in bed, thinking about what happened. What was that? I closed my eyes, envisioning the scene of the cutting. At first I thought she was afraid of the blood. It could have brought memories back. But as I dug deeper, I remembered the blood dripping from her eyes. What was that? Was it some kind of disorder? She couldn't be. But what if she was?

Just then as I was thinking, a giant boom of thunder and rain erupted in the sky. I closed the bedroom window then lay back down. Oh, how I loved the rain. I found it peaceful.

As shades of purples lit up my room, I saw something I hadn't seen before in the pitch blackness of the room. A man was standing in the far corner. I sat back up against the headboard, eyes wide.

The man moved. His hands went to his belt. *Click!* went the metal as it was unbuckled. My heart thumped in my chest. I knew what he was going to do to me.

I sat there unblinking. This was it. I would die tonight. I deserved it anyway.

Finally, the man lunged at me.

I fell on the floor. Sunlight was shining through my window. It was only a dream. Thank god. My heart slowed down a little. I run my hands across my face and through my hair, letting out a breath. When I pull them back, I saw upon my palm a splatter of red.

With that, I ran to the bathroom. Looking in the mirror, I saw that maybe it had been somewhat real. There, underneath my eye, was a giant bruise. Some of my skin broke through, beading crimson.

I fixed myself up and tried to think of what happened. I knew who did it. I didn't have to question that.

It was ten, too late for school. I didn't want to go anyway, not anymore. They wouldn't be suspended forever, and I knew they wouldn't stop hurting me. There was no point to anyway. I had no future.

Maybe Viper didn't go to school. Could I talk to her? I had to at least try.

I went to the house and knocked on the door. No answer. There were no cars either. I was about to leave, but then I heard the faint sound of music coming from the garden.

When I got to the gazebo, I saw that there was no one there, but the record was still spinning. Beside it I saw a piece of paper flapping in the wind. It read:

Dear Damian,

I know you're probably confused but I told you all along that we can't be friends. I'm sorry Damian. I wish we could but you wouldn't understand. Stay away from me...forever. Goodbye Damian ~ Viper

I screamed and tore the letter to shreds. Tears filled my eyes. Now I was alone again. There was no one left. Miles thought I was a freak now. If my band friends knew, they wouldn't understand me. I lost the one girl I actually loved. There was no one left. The others would keep hurting me, and I couldn't deal with that anymore. She probably moved, leaving me alone with this mess. If the others didn't get me, the cops would lock me up for something I didn't do. My life was over.

I ran home, slamming the door behind me. I had to do this. I couldn't waste another second. I went to my father's room first, taking his box then I took the one from mine. I then locked myself in the bathroom.

First I freed Isabel from her box. There was no need for her to be here, just like me. She was finally healed, so I let her fly away out the window.

Before I began writing, I looked at all the happy pictures I had. Hopefully, I would have that again. Picking up the pen I wrote:

To whom it may concern:

My name is Damian Winters. I'm 16 years of age. By the time you read this I'll be dead. I'm sorry if this hurts you, whoever you may be, but I've made up my mind. I can't fight this anymore. I have no friends and my father beats me. At school everyone hates me. So that is why I must go. I have to be with the people I love. There is nothing left for me here. I'm sorry...

I dropped the pen, tears rushing down my face. My whole body was shaking, trembling. Tears welled up and blurred my vision so much I couldn't see. I had to do this. There was no other choice.

I take out the pistol in my father's box. I felt a certain satisfaction as I held it in my hand. *This is it. Good-bye.* I put the barrel to my head and closed my eyes. With the click of the safety, I slowly squeezed the trigger. Then there was a loud bang.

AM I DEAD?

Damian

Perhaps I was supposed to feel it, the bullet through my head. Perhaps I was supposed to see it, the gleaming white light. But there was nothing. No feeling at all. Only the reds of my eyelids were visible. Something wasn't right. Was I truly dead?

I felt someone grabbed my hand. I took in a deep breath, still breathing. My eyes opened, and before me was my bathroom sink. Liquid stained my cheeks. *I am still alive.*

I couldn't believe it. I almost killed myself!

I turned my head to see her. She was crying, red from her eyes. I paid no attention to where the gun went but to her as she embraced me.

"I'm sorry. I'm so sorry, Damian," she said to me. "I'll never leave you again."

Tears never streamed harder down my face. She held me and I felt safe. I breathe in her smell, consumed her warmth as I cried into her neck. After a few minutes, she did something I never thought she'd do.

At first she wiped my tears with the tips of her thumbs. Her eyes looked into mine. There was no thought in me as she pressed her lips against mine. It was light at first but then her tongue pushed through the seams of my lips. We kissed like we never had before, and I stopped crying. I had a feeling in my heart as though it was being repaired, as though everything would be all right again forever.

When we pulled away, she ran her fingers through my bangs, staring me in the eyes once more. I never thought a stare could be so nice. I was not afraid of those eyes. They were such reassuring, beautiful eyes.

Her lips parted as she said something I never thought she would say, "I love you, Damian."

"I love you too," I croaked and we kissed.

I AM SIMPLY DEAD

A beam of light broke through the ceiling, shining down on the floor. My eyes glanced to that light for a few minutes now. When I looked at it, I felt a change. But only a tiny beam within complete darkness. I felt it now, the light beside me, the only flame keeping me alive.

She laid her head upon my shoulder, running her hands among my chest. Her thumb traced tiny circles, which sent butterflies throughout my stomach. Every now and then, I felt her lips press against my neck.

I remember the day she showed me her scars, but ever since then, they disappeared. I traced back all that I could: "It's best if we are not friends," she had said; out of school a lot, sick?; "damned"; the blood in her eyes; how her chest was barely rising as she lay next to me now.

"Viper," I managed to speak.

"Yes."

I waited a few seconds, putting my words together. "What are you?"

No answer.

"Are you a vampire or something?"

I heard a staggered breath and could feel her smile. "No, I'm not a vampire. Not quite. I've been dead a very long time. Even when I was alive." She paused. "You don't want to know these things about me, Damian."

"But I do." I turned my head to look at her the best I can. "You're not evil, Viper."

"But I am."

"No." And she looked up at me. "You could have walked away, could have let me die. You chose me the day you met me. You should have stayed away but you didn't. Why?"

"Because you're more like me than you realize." She traces my cheek. Then glanced to my lips and back to my eyes. There was pain in her eyes. "You're dead, Damian."

I lay unthinking. I was lost, not understanding what she meant. I didn't understand anything for that matter. What was happening to my life? What was happening to me? Perhaps she hadn't said what I thought she said, but she did.

"Are you saying that I really did..." I staggered. My arms and lips began to tremble.

"No." A tear streamed down her cheek. "You were dying the day you first dreamt of death. And now I'm afraid it's too late. You wandered too far. Now you are like me."

"No you're wrong," I said, confused. "There's no way I could be dead and not know it. You're crazy."

I pushed away from her. *How could I have been in love with this?* I had to be dreaming. None of this had happened. I was back in my room, listening to music, never heard of the Johanssons.

I stared at her. She seemed hurt. I did not give in though. One part of me thought she was a murderer. And suddenly, the image of Halloween came to mind. Not the bodies hanging but of when she came out of the woods. The blood that stained her dress was real, wasn't it?

She tried to calm me down as my breath becomes uncontrolled and heavy.

"Stay away from me," I found myself saying.

But no. I need you. I love you, but I don't understand. Is it wrong to love you?

"Damian," she said. Somehow I end up in her arms again. "I'm not going to hurt you." She planted a kiss on top of my head. "I know you're scared, but you are here. Everything is going to be okay."

"If I'm dead," I said, "then what am I?"

"Very much like me," she said. "That's what I feared all along." There was a pause. "You don't have to stay with me. If you leave, I understand." Then she mumbled something I wasn't supposed to hear, "Everyone leaves."

"I want to stay," I said and I kissed her.

"Damian, we need to talk," said Miles, practically yelling.

It was the next day, and I just had gotten home about a few minutes ago. Wolfe was rubbing herself against my calves, an expression on her face as though she knew what had been going on.

"Calm down, Miles," I said on the phone as I opened the fridge, but everything looked quite unappetizing.

"Calm down! How could I calm down! I heard what happened, about you trying to kill yourself. I'm sorry. I'm not yelling at you, Damian. There is nothing to be ashamed of. Please, let's just talk this out."

He was dropping his tone, and I heard choking in his voice. I stood there for a moment, fridge wide open, listening to him crying. How could I have been so selfish?

"I'm sorry, Miles," I said truthfully. I let out a deep breath.

"Why, Damian?"

Great, a question I couldn't answer. I wanted to let out everything, but I knew that I couldn't.

"I can't talk about it. Not now, please." I closed the fridge.

"At least tell me how you are doing. Don't lie to me. Don't you dare!"

I honestly didn't know. I wasn't sitting there with a gun to my head, but I wasn't exactly skipping down the street. I was simply living for the sake of someone else, Viper. About to break any second of her leaving. "I'll be okay, Miles. If you want to, I could go down today. Just pick me up."

"Are you ever going back to school? You know you have to."

"No," I denied, not wanting to be in that dreadful place again. "I'm never going back."

"Damian," he whined, "we can fix this."

"Great, but I'm not going back," I stated. "Just me and the band now."

He was there again. Jace. It was strangely hot today, so I wore a short-sleeved shirt and shorts. I had felt so uncomfortable. First off, Jace was gorgeous. Second, he could see all of my scars, healing but still.

Miles kept his smiling face as always. We didn't mention the incident to my surprise. Instead, we pretty much played video games.

"Headshot," said Miles, getting one off of Jace.

"Ah. Fuck you."

"With pleasure," said Miles.

My eyes became twice the size. Fingers still moving, I looked at Miles. Jace was also looking at Miles, but Miles was glued to the TV, an expression of concentration on his face.

"What," he said to Jace, still looking at the TV. "He doesn't give a shit."

I couldn't believe it. Miles and Jace were together. I didn't know Miles was gay.

"So what about you, Damian?" said Miles after a few minutes. "You got a boyfriend yet?"

I pondered for a moment, wondering if he was joking. How could he have known? I don't remember telling him I was bi.

"No," I said.

"That's right. You a ladies man."

"I got *a* girl. That's all." A smile on my face. "Are you drunk?"

"Hardly."

Silence. Then Jace shouted, "About freaking time!" I nearly spat out the Gatorade I was taking a sip of. Then Jace began to sing, and

I couldn't hold in my laughter. "Tea-bagging your dead body. Tea-bagging your dead body."

After the video games, we went to Vick's house. I couldn't believe I almost missed this day out of my own stupidity.

THE DEAD

Damian

We had a lot of laughs at Vick's house. So much so, I was smiling when I got off of the public bus. It would have been late if Miles had driven me, I didn't want to be rude.

Earbuds plugged in, hoodie on my head, walking throughout the night, it felt like the old times again but less depressing. I was starting to think then, as the sound of guitars drowned my music, that maybe just maybe I could make sense of things. I just had to sit down, figure all this out, and everything would be okay. Everything would be fine like she told me it would as I thought through life though it made less sense.

Hello, my name is Damian. (Hi, Damian). And I tried to kill myself. My mother is dead. I guess I learned from her. Just like her, I couldn't deal with the pain. My father abuses me. I guess I learned from him. I have scars deeper than any words ever said. I get constantly bullied by my classmates. I guess I learned from them. Every night I am wide awake, my thoughts playing with my head. I once felt love, but yet it is alien. I loved my mother when she was alive, a happy, caring woman, but she was taken away from me. I loved a boy, someone who accepted me, but we couldn't be together, so he was taken away. Now I love a girl. I don't even know what she is, who she is, if her name is even her name. She tells me she is dead. I am dead too. But if that is true, how do people see me? How am I still here? What will happen to me?

I was crying now, my eyes fixed to the ground. Visions of blades in my head. *Go away. Please just go away.* I said I would never do it again.

I'm not sure what happened then, but as I was walking passed the cemetery I could have sworn I saw something in the corner of my eyes. My thoughts stopped as did my body. The music on my iPod skipped. My breath was visible, a white cloud of vapor. I then slowly turned my head.

There standing among a sea of stones was a woman. She wore a floral dress, hair pulled back, a smile on her face. It was my mother. A light shined around her, happiness, as though she was there, real and alive.

"Damian," she said.

I closed my gaping mouth, not sure what to do. Before I could think, I found my feet edging toward her. As I neared close, the light around her got bigger, and I found myself no longer in the cemetery. It was gone along with the rest of the night. Now I was in the kitchen of my old home.

A new emotion washed over me. I felt like crying and smiling at the same time. Could she really been here or was I dreaming?

She took her hands in mine. Her skin was cold and light like she was not at all there.

"Oh, my boy. You're so grown up." She put a hand to my cheek. "It's been so long."

As I looked from her smile to her eyes, I saw it, a flash of gold in a sea of blue. Where had I seen that before?

"I never left you, Damian. Not completely," she said, "I never meant to. I know there are things you may not understand right now, but in time you will." As she spoke, I saw more of the gold. *Isabel.* "It is not your time, Damian. You still have a life to live. I love you, son." A tear streamed down my cheek. "There is nothing wrong with you. I wish I could have come to you sooner, but you always shut me out." She placed a kiss on my cheek. "Trust her. She knows the truth."

I don't remember what happened after she left. I only remembered the voices. I saw the evil faces. I had gone to a place within my mind so dark and evil, a place no one should ever see. But as I was there, I was not in danger anymore. The warmth of my mother's presence filled me.

Next thing I know, I could feel my body again. I did not open my eyes. I felt the ground underneath me. Something cold covered my skin, and I know that it is finally here—winter's first snow.

SELL MY SOUL

Slayer

The murders weren't stopping. Of course, they weren't. The murderer was still up and about. I told the sheriff of my suspicions, but he seemed to object, and the newspapers never worked. It was as if no one had read them. Not even the slightest peep was heard. People still seemed clueless of who committed the crime. I wasn't crazy. I remembered making the papers, throwing them at people's doorsteps. Had they somehow magically disappeared before anyone got them?

I wasn't sure of much besides (a) these murders are happening, (b) I know who the culprits are and my mission is to kill them, (c) the sheriff is a dumb pain in the ass, and (d) I need to get rid of him.

It was nightfall, and I was walking through the woods, flashlight in hand. They would be in here somewhere. If I found them, I would kill them on the spot these sick bastards.

Just as I was walking, I heard the sound of a tree branch snapping. I whirled around, gun in hand. I saw nothing, but I heard it again from behind a tree. I edged forward. My flashlight was dying; it became dimmer.

Slowly I walked, trying not to make noise. I heard the sound of chewing as I got to the tree. Suddenly my flashlight went off. I heard it just a few feet before me. The munching and cracking got louder. I accidently let out a whine, and the sounds stopped. I felt my heart beat faster. *It is staring at me, the murderer. This is it.* Nothing happened. I was afraid to slap the flashlight awake.

There was a few seconds of silence as I did not move. I lifted my flashlight. It felt like an eternity until it hit my palm. I quickly covered the light with my hand. Pointing it in the direction of the murderer I let go to see that it was a deer.

It stared at me for a moment then ran away. At first I thought it was because of me, but then I heard it again, the snapping of tree branches behind me. I slowly turned to see a figure in a black cloak staring at me. A long curved sword was held in its hand, perfect for slitting someone's throat. My eyes never left the being. I was so frightened; I had forgotten my gun was there.

This couldn't be who I was looking for. Something inside me told me it was far worse. The being sniffed the air and said in a low demonic voice, "I can just smell the fear on you. But there is something else too, demise perhaps. Sell your soul, and I'll help you, troubled one. Refuse and you die."

That's the night I sold my soul to the devil.

THE CONCERT

Damian

I woke up with the feeling of warmth. I was covered in a sea of blankets in a bedroom that was not mine. Viper's room.

Sun rays beaming through the curtain shined on me. *How come it took me so long to see the beauty in the light?*

From what I could see, it must be noon. A quiet noon. *What happened last night?* I slid my body out the door and down the stairs.

I found her in the kitchen cooking up lunch, hot soup.

"I figured you were cold, asleep in the snow and all," she said without turning to look at me.

How did she see me standing there? I did feel cold, shaking where I stood.

"What is happening to me?" I asked, running my fingers through my hair.

She placed a bowl of soup on the table and responded, "It's part of your process. Everything—the vomiting, the nightmares, seeing/hearing things are all part of it. There is nothing wrong with you. Your depression I can't promise will leave when you turn, but I can try to make you happy," she paused, biting her lip, "She was real, Damian. She was there."

"How do you always know what has happened?" I asked, slightly scared. "How come you were always there when things were going wrong?"

"It's one of my gifts. I can see a person's life story just by looking through their eyes. You invited me in without knowing, Damian. Now I always know where you are. I can't see you, but I know when something bad is going to happen to you. I'll protect you; you don't have to worry anymore."

I felt a little at ease. That explained a lot about the things that happened, how she knew when I needed protection. *No one can hurt you now,* she seemed to somehow say through my mind.

There were a few minutes of silence as I ate my soup when I remembered something. With shocked eyes, I cursed.

"I have a gig tonight."

"Well then, time for some fun."

Inside strobe and disco lights were blinking. Some god awful dubstep was blaring. Everyone had their arms in the air, dancing around. As we peered from behind the curtain, Vick was shaking. He was totally freaked out.

"I can't do this, Damian. I can't," he said while hyperventilating.

"Hey, calm down," I said, taking Vick's shoulders. "It's going to be okay. Okay? We are going to do great."

For some reason, I had some odd inner confidence tonight. I couldn't explain how weird it felt. It was like Vick and I completely traded places. I had never seen him a nervous wreck.

"You're right, mate," said Australian Vick calming down. "We can do this. Get them colored contacts on."

We got out on stage, and cheers erupted from the crowd for they had been waiting for entertainment. I just hope this was what they wanted. There were a few awkward seconds of me standing there as the guys set up. I scanned the crowd, looking for her; and there she was, smiling. I waved with one hand, and with the other, bringing the microphone up to my face.

"How's it going, Camberg!" I yelled and got an eruption of shouts. I never thought that that moment would feel so good. It was as though they were enthused to see me. Of course, half of them were probably drunk.

"We are The Demonic Eyes," I shouted. "We rise from the depths of hell to interfere with your conscious mind."

The bass and guitar started followed by the drums. I banged my head wildly to the beat, and people began to jump up and down. After a few beats, I began to sing.

Sometime through the song, I looked into Viper's eyes. She smiled. In that moment, I had never felt more alive in my life, so sane. It was her that kept me alive; she saved me. I owe her everything. And I thought back to the day when I was sitting in class and she walked in. I thought back to that rainy night, of the car pulling up to me. How different it was then. Now I have her. She was all mine. The thought made me smile.

"Thank you, ladies and gentleman, for coming out here tonight," I said after the last song. "Hope you all come see us again. Now let's fucking party."

I let out a roar, and the crowd went crazy. They started shouting "Demonic Eyes" over and over again even after we left the stage.

"That was awesome," yelled an excited Vick, jumping out at me. "How about now we go home and celebrate with some pizza."

"Sorry, Vick," I said, walking by him. "I've got a girl to see. Later."

I was not even looking at him. I ran into the crowd of people. A slow song began to play. There I found Viper. She wrapped her arms around me, pulling me close as we swayed back and forth.

"Great job tonight," she said.

"It was all right," I said, cutting a smile.

We were so close, and suddenly we were kissing. Her lips were so soft and tasted of cherry. I couldn't believe they were mine forever. She wrapped her fingers in my hair, pulling me closer.

It wasn't the kissing, it wasn't the dancing or holding me close that made me feel loved. She never left me. Even in my worst hour, she came back for me. She came back because I mattered. She wasn't ashamed of me. Maybe perhaps if she could love me, I could love myself too.

Through a kiss I whispered, "I love you. I don't care what you are if you're good or evil or even really Viper Johansson. I love you and will never try to leave you again."

We were walking down the street hand in hand. Cars rushed passed us. I could see my breath before me in a cloud of fog, but Viper didn't seem the slightest bit cold.

"I'm not, you know," she said.

"Hmm?"

"I'm not who you think I am," she said. "It's all a disguise, the me you used to know."

"I know," I said. "I'd like to know you if I can."

"Of course, you can," she said.

"Are you sure or are we better off not friends?" I asked jokingly, bringing her to me.

"Funny," she deadpanned.

"We need to start over? We need to leave here. Don't you feel it?"

"Yes. Things are going to change quite soon."

The sound of an engine running was heard behind us. I turned and looked to see a black Cadillac sitting in the middle of the road. No other car was in sight.

"It's the sheriff," I whispered to her, but I have no idea how I knew that.

"Run," she said.

We hit the cement of the sidewalk, the sound of our feet pounding. The car chased after us. She was so fast, I didn't think I could keep up, but she grabbed my arm with a tense pressure, and somehow, we seemed to be going the same speed. The wind was gushing around me, the poles and houses a blur. Before I knew it, we were in the woods and in our hideaway, door slammed shut.

In a few minutes, we are on the bed, lying there, staring at the ceiling, hands hugging.

"What is your name?" asked Viper, accepting my request to start over.

"Damian. Damian Winters. What is your name?"

There was a moment of silence then she said, "My name is Skylar. Skylar Maxx."

"Well, Skylar," I said, "I know we just met and all, but I think I may be taking a fancy to you."

She laughed then began to kiss me. "Oh, Damian. What am I going to do with you?" she asked during kissing.

She completely stopped for a moment and looked at me. Her eyes were so sad. "I will tell you everything if you tell me."

I told her about my mother, about my father, and my bullies, about Carver, everything. She didn't comment, didn't interrupt. We just lay there staring up at the ceiling, but I knew she was listening.

"Do you think he's coming back?"

"No," I said. "I don't think he ever will…not after what he did. Not after he said he never would again."

I felt her fingers intertwine with mine. "Then stay with me, with us, and I'll show you what's like to live. You have power, Damian. You don't even know what you are capable of. You could get your revenge on them. All of them."

"I don't want to kill people."

"You don't have to, but you can make them suffer like you did. Give yourself time to think about it."

I looked at her. *Is she crazy?* Maybe she was. Maybe it was what she was that made her. I was in love with her either way. No one could take her away from me.

"I told you, Damian. I'm a bad person."

"Then tell me…your story."

EXORCISM

The door was as wide as the opening of my mouth as I appeared amid the rubble. The walls were spray painted curse words. Pictures were broken, tables flipped over, papers scattered the floor. Everything was in ruins.

On the living room wall was a symbol of a skull and crossbones painted on thick and slimy red. I put my hand to it to see if I could rub it off. It came back a dark crimson on my hands, blood.

This couldn't have been them. Could it?

"It wasn't," said a voice behind me. Skylar. *How is she able to do that? Get inside my head?* "There have been some people following us. One of the reasons why we came here is an entity. He masks himself as Death. The same entity has been haunting my family for years. I don't know what he wants with us. I do not know what he wants with you, but now I have no choice. I must teach you everything even before you turn."

"I'm not understanding," I said. "I have three people out to kill me."

"Us," she interrupted. "But apparently, one is more interested in you. And yes, you're half demon like me, us."

"How do you, how do you know everything?" I slightly pulled at my hair, puzzled.

She pointed to the kitchen wall. In blood were the words: "I'm coming for you. Damian."

"Pack your stuff. We need to go," was all she said, and she walked out the door.

I got the things that I would need. I left behind all my pictures, except one of my mother's and kept the box. Those things I could never throw away.

That was when I realized, where was Wolfe?

I checked every room, the second floor, first, even the basement. She wasn't there. I began to panic. Where could she be? Perhaps she had run off when the havoc happened. She was gone, completely gone. I just hoped she was in a better place, with a family that could take care of her, and that she was not actually out on the streets.

"Well, Wolfe, good luck," I said and closed the front door.

"Let me see your eyes," said Tom.

We were in their home library. We had just told him pretty much everything. By the end of our story, he looked scared, slightly.

As he was playing around with my eyelids and lower parts of the eye, he said, "The name's Alaric by the way. The jerk head over there is Hunter."

"Thanks, Dad," he muttered.

When he was awkwardly done doing whatever it was he was doing to me, he sighed. "He changes tonight."

Hunter had an expression on his face like he was about to shit himself. Skylar was expressionless as stone.

"Well, fuck," said Hunter. "What are we going to do?"

"We're going to have to do a ritual to speed up the process and cleanse him so he doesn't come back evil," he stated as though it was the most normal thing to say. Then to me, "Have you ever cut so deep that you don't think stitches could possibly fix it, and it burns like hell?"

"Umm…sorta, yeah."

"Not to pressure you," he said, his eyes never moving, a tad creepy smile appearing on his face, "but this is going to hurt a lot worse. Like it's all over your body, cutting from the inside out."

"Umm...," was all I could say, terrified.

"I know you're scared, but know that it will eventually end," he said. "People are all made up of demons and angels inside, but on this night, the demon gets more power in hope of taking over your soul. I know it sounds terrifying, but it's going to be all right in the end, okay?"

I nodded my head, not really sure what to think of this. I was just dumbfounded.

"I want you to fight it. If you feel like it's taking over, you got to fight. All right?"

I nodded my head once more.

They brought me to a room behind a wall of books. It was completely empty except for a door on the back wall and a small table in the far corner. The walls were made of stone; the floor, a slab of concrete, dirty. The room was quite dark except for a few candles burning on the floor. Skylar wrapped my body with rope, tying me to a chair.

Behind her, Alaric and a priest were talking. They seemed as though they knew each other for a long time. This was really happening. I was about to be exorcised.

"It's going to be okay," said Skylar, kissing my lips. She looked once more at me then covered my head with a cloth. Everything was barely visible.

"Let's get started," said Alaric. He then spoke, not aloud, but in my head. "I welcome you, my boy, with open arms. I should have seen it in you. My blood is your blood, and in our blood, you shall stand... son."

Anxiety was rushing through my body, filling my veins like poison. My limbs were shaking from nerves. This couldn't be happening but it was. Two months I was being beat up wanting to die. Today I would die but not at all the way I had intended.

As I sat there, it was all too quiet. I jumped slightly. A jolt went through my body. A stinging sensation was traveling throughout my veins. I began sweating, my skin burning. It was as if fire had been in my blood.

I began to scream, my fist clenching. The priest began to bellow words in Latin.

It was as if whatever was inside me hated to hear it for blood splattered out of my mouth. There was something moving inside my stomach, ripping at my insides.

My screams seem to diminish from a high pitch to low in a matter of seconds. It was a scratchy, eerie sound. It couldn't have been me.

I began to shake the chair, my nails clawing into the wood, fingertips bleeding. As blood streamed from my eyes, I heard Skylar's words.

"It is okay, Damian. You can fight this."

My mind went blank.

I awoke in a bed, Skylar's. A wet cloth lay on my head. I felt her lips skimmed my neck; her arms wrapped around me. I feel nothing but a tingling sensation in my stomach. It was as if nothing ever happened.

"You passed out after ten minutes. You had it easy. How do you feel?"

"All right," I answered and kissed her.

She smiled.

"What?"

"Nothing. You're just so cute." Cute she said as familiar as ever. We went downstairs to see Alaric.

"Good morning. Didn't expect you to be up," said Alaric cheerfully as he sharpened a knife with a rock while watching the football game.

"I think I need some explanation."

"Another day," said Alaric, eyes still on the TV. He set down his knife and went through his wallet. He handed me a wad of green and a set of keys. "Take her out. Have some fun…but not too much."

He went to his knife. I gulped, "Thanks."

"Do you ever…you know, find anything weird about the house?"

"Not at all. Why? Just the garden thing?"

We were walking down the street hand in hand in the city of Camberg. There were a lot of stores, and movie theaters, plays, but we weren't quite sure where to go yet.

"Well, a lot happened in that house. I don't know exactly what but…"

"The room you know we were in," she brought down her voice to a whisper and said, "there used to be satanic rituals."

"Oh," I said. "Well, that's a great place to…you know. You could have let things inside of me."

"Not quite. They were already sentenced back to hell," she said then changing the subject, she pointed at a sign. "It's my favorite band."

Camberg was probably the most confusing place ever geographically. Behind a strip of advertising offices was a park, and behind the park were a bar and a few newspaper corporations right smack in the middle of the land. Behind that was a field, and in that field was a stage.

As we stood there watching the stage, waiting for the concert to start, I realized that this was my first. How pathetic did that feel? Almost seventeen years old and I've never been to a concert. Well, it's about time.

Two guys stood next to us, one with an arm around the other. The guy being practically hugged was shivering. Not a thought of Carver came to my mind but only the thought that I wasn't cold. Not the slightest breeze sent a chill down my spine. Was I really dead inside?

Several cheers hit the crowd, and the concert began.

Sometime through the concert, I ended up crowd surfing. Just then as I was up in the air above all the bodies, I heard a drone and a whistle. It was faint under the sound of the music but I heard it. I knew what was coming. There in the distance was the sheriff and his accomplices running through the crowd.

"Put me down," I said in a panic. "Put me down."

I was put somewhat safely down. A few people looked at me perplexed, as if to say, "What's your problem," but I paid no attention. I kept onward, pushing my way through the bodies until I found Skylar. We broke free and dashed down the hill.

RUN FOR YOUR LIFE

We got in the car, and I hit the pedal as fast as I can.

"We have to ditch the car," said Skylar more nonchalantly than she should. Perhaps she was out of breath.

"Tell me what's going on," I nearly shouted, changing the subject. "You're not really clear on anything. No more vague answers. Tell me what is happening."

"I told you we are being chased."

"Yes, but why?"

"The humans think we killed those people. The Deathmaster wants us dead, on the other hand, because we won't join him."

"Join him in what?"

"Not sure. But he has something evil planned."

I tell her about the incident in the library. "Does he have anything to do with that?"

"Something happened in our house a long time ago. Perhaps it was a mistake to move there, but we hadn't known he had been so close. Like we were turned, the people that lived there were trying to be turned, but they tried to escape. They were killed. I think there is a greater purpose for all of this, yet no one ever knows his intentions. You see, fear is a game for him. Why are you so interested in the house anyway?"

"Because now all of this is my reality. There is no going back now," I answered.

The sirens got louder, and the blur of the vehicle hit the front mirror.

"Go faster."

"If I go any faster, we'll crash."

I turned the steering wheel as I got to an intersection, pulling dust behind me and sped in the direction of the highway. The police car wasn't able to stop fast enough, going pass us in another direction. He tried to swerve, hitting a telephone pole.

"Yeah. Fuck the police," I yelled.

I had never been more enthused.

We burst through the double doors of the house and hurried into the library. Alaric looked up and dropped his book, sensing something wrong.

"Darling, what is the matter," he asked Skylar.

"They are coming for us. We must flee from here."

"How long have we got?" he asked, getting up abruptly.

"Less than a half an hour."

"Pack," he nearly shouted. "Hurry. Let's go."

YOU CAN RUN BUT YOU CAN'T HIDE

I rushed up the stairs with Skylar by my side. I pulled two suitcases from the closet, one for her, one for me. That would have to do. We didn't want to bring so much with us. We didn't have much time either.

We packed anything useful and hurried out the door. I expected things to be quiet, normal like always. So it was until I closed the truck and heard a scream.

"Mrs. Henderson," I shouted.

I dashed across the street, Skylar with me. There Wolfe was crying and scratching at the front door. I burst through, my heart beating fast.

There above her was a man. His face was covered with a hat, eye holes cut out. He glanced up at us. A dagger stained with blood was held in his hand. I looked into his eyes and recognized them, but whose eyes were they.

Without thinking, I launched myself at the man. Running toward him, he disappeared into nothing. He was gone, disappeared into thin air.

I stopped, using my heels, nearly falling backward. I knew that had to be the slayer. Now he was going to find me, but why did he disappear?

I went to her. She was cut, bleeding at the throat. Her eyes looked to me. She was dead, gone forever.

"I'm sorry," I whispered and closed her eyes.

"We must hurry," said Skylar. "They are coming."

"Indeed, my love," I said, a hollow feeling in my chest.

We fled outside and saw sirens flashing on the reflection of the snow.

"Hop in," said Alaric, his tires skidding on the concrete, "now."

I let Viper in first then hopped in, nearly feeling a bullet graze my arm.

"Hang onto your seats," said Alaric, hitting the gas.

He zoomed down the street, the police not far behind. We cut onto the highway. Shots were decreasing in fear of hitting others. We did not stop; we kept moving on. We were getting farther away from them, leaving smoke in our path, but then it happened.

It seemed as though time slowed. It felt as though a few seconds was a minute. Alaric looked through the rearview mirror, tracking the enemy, eyes no longer on the road. A police man hung his hand out the window and shot, hitting the back left tire of the Camaro.

We went skidding, turning into the median. Alaric tried to step on the brakes, causing us to flip over. Alaric swore. Skylar screamed. The windows imploded, shattering everywhere. I smacked my head on the top of the car. This was it. I had to be dead, but I wasn't, not yet.

The police slowed down, coming toward us.

"Look, I'm stuck. My arm may be broken," said Alaric. "Hunter is unconscious. You must take my daughter. Run into the forest. Go!"

I tried unbuckling her seatbelt, but it wouldn't budge. I tugged at it, snapping it in half. She was still alive when I pulled her out and started heading for the forest.

I did not flinch, did not hesitate as shots were fired after me, as I broke through the forest. I kept running until I was sure they were gone and laid her on the ground. Her lips were stained with blood. I feared she was dead, but then I brushed my fingers through her hair, causing her to snap awake.

"Where are we?" she asked.

"The forest," I said. "Your father and brother could not make it."

"Are they dead?"

"Not the least," I answered, and her face calmed. "They can't capture them. They'll find a way of getting out."

"What does that mean for us?"

"I'm not sure. For once, I'm not sure."

We were walking through the forest, snow crunching underneath our boot soles. I hadn't felt the least bit cold even only in a short-sleeved tee shirt.

"We can't go back for them," she said, "We can't risk being caught because then no one would be able to save us."

"We can't stay here either," I said. "You told me never to come here at night. Is that because of *him*?"

"Yes," she said. "We must get to safe area for the night and soon. Take my hand."

I took her hand. I don't even know how she knew where she was going, but with the speed of lightning, we ended up at our secret place.

Viper was horrified, I too completely a gasp. It was completely vandalized. The door was broken down. Words were spray-painted across it in an unknown language.

"They are coming for us," she said and grabbed my hand.

We appeared in front of the house and hurried through the door.

"We must hide."

We went down the halls, through the library, through the empty room I was exorcised in. We found ourselves staring at the strange door.

"We'll be safe. The devils are gone from here," said Skylar.

Behind the door was a long corridor made of stone. On the ceiling were mirrors. Everything was dark and smelled of must. We hid in the far corner of the corridor underneath a table.

It came quicker than I thought it would. I could hear it so clearly, the creak of the front door opening so far away. It was completely heart pounding that they could actually get that bolted door open. Then I heard the sound of the footsteps, heavy boots hitting the floor.

She grabbed my hand so tight and looked at me. "Listen, Damian. He is coming for you. Not me. I will help you, but no matter what I do, I cannot kill him. You must or he'll just come back. He is your nightmare, Damian. You must destroy him."

I kissed her softly. "I will," I found myself saying.

I knew who the slayer was. I heard it in the stomping of the boot soles. I saw it in his eyes looking up at me. It was time I ended it.

"Don't move," I demanded. "Stay where you are until he is gone. I must do this on my own."

After all this time, it would finally end. I knew Skylar enough since the time she stood up to Billy. She would not let me do it on my own, which is why I did something to her. I don't really know how I did it. I just did. It was like because I wanted it, it happened just as I wanted.

"Do not move from where you sit," I said again. I could feel a change in my eyes. They were spiraling, swirling, but how? "Not until he is dead."

I let go of her and stood in the middle of the room unarmed. I clenched my fist, waiting as I heard the door in the other room. Then the footsteps sounded louder, and adrenaline pumped through my veins as I stared at the door.

Come on. What are you, scared? You are nothing but a coward.

The doorknob turned, and the door creaked open. There I came face to face with the slayer.

"Oh," he said with a delighted tone. "You changed so much, my boy."

AND SO THE DICE ROLLS

"What a surprise, father," I said, shaking slightly. "Such a surprise you hadn't killed me sooner. Why was that? You're afraid of me, aren't you? Either that or you are a coward."

The man grinned and chuckled. A giant scar covered his eye I had never seen before. That is not a thing you can cover up. "Aren't you spiteful now. You knew it was me but for how long?" When I didn't answer. "You know you are a lot like your mother. She put up quite a fight."

My blood never flowed faster through my veins. Heat rose within my body, sweat dripping from my brow. "Don't you fucking talk about her."

"You should have heard her, Damian. The way she screamed. You never screamed. You always pleaded for help. Let's see what you do now."

He takes out a dagger, long and sharp, from his back pocket. My eyes never left him. *How could I get the dagger from him? This is not a fair game.*

He swung his right hand toward my side. I tried to step back, but he was swift, causing the blade to slash through my skin. I yelped and Skylar shouted.

"Oh, you got a female with you too," he said. "How sweet."

He swung, aiming for my head, and I ducked. I charged into him, his hand still in midair. I knocked him to the ground. I got a good grip on his wrist, trying to get the dagger, but he pushed me off, sending me flying in the air. The wind hit me, and I felt out of breath as I hit the floor with a smack.

I was about to get up, but he grabbed me, burying me into the wall. I couldn't breathe as his hands grasped my neck.

"Looks like it is the end of you, son. At last."

I spat at him and brought my knee up to his crotch. He cursed and stumbled back, accidently letting go of the dagger. It fell. I grabbed it. I sliced at the man, first cutting his arm. He took his other arm, his fist coming toward my face. I pulled an upper cut, the blade connecting with his torso before his fist hit me. He then collapsed.

"This is for my mother," I said, feeling a tear stream down my cheek.

I raised the dagger above my head and brought it down. It stabbed him through the chest where his frozen heart would be. I kept stabbing after that. I don't know for how long, but I just wanted to make sure he was dead.

That is when I turned around and embraced her. *It is over. He is really gone. No one could ever hurt me now. We could run away together. Oh gosh! She is the greatest thing that had ever happened to me.* Yet I was still afraid, running through what I had done in my head.

I do believe I truly died that day. I was gone, my last breath taken in. I was something new, something dead. Perhaps in the end I had everything as I wanted it to be, just not as I had imagined it to be. *So the dice rolls, turning on its side. Evens are for good. Odds are for evil.*

Down the stairs of life it goes, determining the final sentence of your fate after death when it comes to a stop. Evens are for heaven, odds are for hell. Which way I was leaning toward now was crystal clear as the glass of humanity shattered.

Everything had happened so fast. One day was different from the rest. There was no doubt I changed. When the leaves fell to the ground, I was powerless, fluttering to the earth, below the branches of strength. Soon seasons did change, transforming into a massive storm. The wind and snow blew rapidly, bringing in the hail. At that very moment in time, I was the hail. I was the oncoming storm.

So the dice rolls, turning on its side. Evens or odd, what is it for you? What is your fate?

Afterword

Dear Reader,

This book is dedicated to no other than you. I would like to thank you for buying my first book and not putting it down until the very end. You have no idea how much it means to me, and it's something I can't fathom well into my dearest gratitude. And for those who haven't read *Bloody Nightmares*, I hope you enjoy this book and make sure to read the other when you get a chance if you love nonstop action and suspense.

    This novel is the beginning of the Prequel series to *World Domination,* and it is especially dedicated to those that have never felt like they belong in this world, to those that are going through really hard times, or to those whom are scared to walk out that door. Whether you have/are being bullied, have/had depression, suicidal thoughts, family issues, eating disorders, and the like, you are not alone. I love every single one of my fans, and I never ever want to hear that one of them decided to take the door out of this world. So if you are dealing with these problems and feel like you have no one to talk to, I suggest calling a hotline of the state/country you reside in. There are so many people who care about you even if you don't realize it. Suicide isn't a solution; it just stops things from ever getting better. Damian would know.

Suicide Hotlines

USA: 18007848433, 18007842433, 18002738255
Argentina: 54-0223-493-0430
Austria: 01-713-3374
Barbados: 429-9999
Belgium: 106
Botswana: 3911270
Brazil: 21-233-9191
Canada: 519-416-486-2242 (Ontario)
1-888-787-2880 (Alberia)
1-866-872-0113 (British Columbia)
514-723-4000 (Quebec)
China: 852-2382-0000
Costa Rica: 506-253-5439
Croatia: 01-4833-888
Cyprus: 357-77-77-72-67
Denmark: 70-201-201
Egypt: 7621602
Finland: 040-5032199
France: 01-45-39-4000
Germany: 0800-181-0721
Holland: 0900-0767
India: 92-22-307-3451
Ireland: 44-0-8457-90-90-90
Italy: 06-705-4444
Japan: 3-5286-9090
Mexico: 525-510-2550
Netherlands: 0900-0767
New Zealand: 4-473-9739
Norway: 47-815-33-300
New Guinea: 675-326-0011
Philippines: 02-896-9191
Poland: 52-70-000
Russia: 8-20-222-82-10
Spain: 91-459-00-50
South Africa: 0861-322-322

Sweden: 031-711-2400
Switzerland: 143
Thailand: 02-249-9977
United Kingdom: 08457-90-90-90
Ukraine: 0487-327715

About the Author

Growing up in a small town in Massachusetts, Jacqueline spends her time when not writing dancing, playing instruments, drowning in a sea load of books, listening to bands, or spending time blogging on the Internet. Being only a teenager, she still attends school and is thinking of ways to succeed in her chosen future career. *The Demonic Eyes* is her first published novel.

CPSIA information can be obtained at www.ICGtesting.com
Printed in the USA
BVOW07s1445180914

367430BV00001B/1/P